CHASING ETERNITY

By

DIANN DUCHARME

ISBN 13: 9798771962863

Other books by Diann Ducharme

The Outer Banks House

Return to the Outer Banks House

Home to the Outer Banks

1

Ryan Abernathy's long legs loped through the last interval of his HIIT session on the treadmill. His eyes trained on the beige wall in front of him, he thought of nothing except his body's health and well-being.

The daily work out completed, Ryan wiped his head and neck with a towel and made his way to the kitchen. Assembling ingredients and piling them into a blender, he stabbed the "puree" button with a determined forefinger.

He ran a hand over his toned torso as he watched the spinach, avocado, apple, Medjool dates, flaxseeds, chia seeds and mint mix rapidly into mush. He made a mental note that a cup contained approximately 200 calories; he could eat another 800 calories today.

He poured the mixture into a glass and carried it to the kitchen table, where his biochemistry textbook waited for him, along with his neatly lined up bottles of vitamins and supplements. He prescribed to a daily regimen that included multivitamins, capsules of fish oils, and supplements of muscadine grape, Coenzyme Q10, turmeric, milk thistle, ashwaganda and bacopa, all of which had been shown to neutralize the free radicals that roamed a body, damaging the body's cells and leading to premature aging.

He washed the capsules down with a glass of water, then popped a tablet of anti-anxiety medication into his mouth and swallowed.

Humming tunelessly, he scooted his stainless steel chair closer to the table and opened the textbook, reading a few paragraphs and analyzing a chart. Then he drained the glass and dropped onto the white linoleum to do some push-ups. He felt so capable, he clapped his hands together after each upward thrust.

At push-up number fifty-three, he heard a knock on his apartment door.

He knew that it was Rose Buxton, a fellow research associate with the genetics of longevity study. She was the only friend whom he had felt comfortable enough asking to drive him to the Dulles airport.

"Ew," she said, eyeing his sweaty t-shirt as she strolled inside. She smelled of a dry October day in Virginia.

"You're early," he noted. "I haven't showered yet."

"Are you packed at least?"

"Almost."

She pulled open the refrigerator door and peered inside. "Looks like a year's supply of tofu in here." She wrenched open the full crisper drawer. "Your vegetables are going to go bad while you're in Ireland, you know."

"You want to take them home with you?"

"Ha ha, very funny."

Ryan smiled. Rose was a happily chubby thirty-year-old medical student, studying to be a pathologist. A year ago, he had been on a date with her, at her insistence, but things hadn't moved forward, probably because she had made the mistake of taking him to an Italian restaurant with an all-you-can-eat buffet.

He had watched anxiously as she devoured at least five slices of some spongy white bread drenched in olive oil, a meal-sized portion of Caesar salad, and a giant bowl of fettucini alfredo. His side garden salad cowered in shock.

After the meal, he had delicately tried to explain to her how eating *small* amounts of food triggered genes that appeared to promote cell survival, improve DNA stability and increase energy production. Calorie restriction had been proven to lengthen lifespans in rodents, worms and other species, and newer data suggested that it worked in primates too. It was, he declared, probably the most effective way of extending the maximum life span in animals.

He had leaned back in his chair, satisfied with his sermon, but Rose had sauntered back to the buffet and selected a thick slice of cherry cheesecake. She had eaten the dessert quickly, and then had ordered a cappuccino to chase it down, all while babbling about television shows that Ryan didn't watch, books of fiction that he wouldn't read.

After the date, Rose and Ryan had agreed to be friends.

Because her father was the director of the longevity research study, she helped out at the office on the weekends. Ryan still wasn't quite sure what she did. And yet, it was Rose who had taken the recent call from Dr. Patrick Fitzgerald, an Irish general practitioner and self-professed genealogy buff.

Dr. Fitzgerald thought the specialized study, with their focus on the genes of long-lived relatives, would be interested in two extremely elderly, identical twin sisters on a remote island off the western coast of Ireland. They lived in two separate homes, right next door to one another, with not even a telephone or a television to connect them to the world outside.

They were "so off the radar," he'd said, "that they may as well be living on Mars."

The young doctor claimed that he'd been calling on the island's patients for over five years now, and the entire island seemed to be comprised mostly of elderly people, who fortunately were still independent enough to abide the lack of a retirement home on the island.

He'd said that one of the twins, Cleona Owen, was terribly sick with pneumonia. He had inquired of her age at that point, and she had admitted, while in the midst of a raging fever, to being over one hundred years old—a centenarian—but she'd seemed confused about her exact age. Even a great-granddaughter who lived with her claimed ignorance of the actual number.

The sister, Catherine Owen, had been confined to her bed for the last few months, claiming exhaustion. She couldn't even answer him, when he'd inquired of her age. He'd left them with some pills, but doubted that either sister would survive until the new year.

A pattern of old age and resiliency on the island—coupled with the fact that the two elderly women were twins, had piqued the director's interest—enough to send Ryan from Virginia to Ireland for five days to investigate, despite the known existence of official age documents.

Centenarian siblings were difficult to find, and even more

difficult to thoroughly validate, but they were the cornerstone of their particular longevity study—"longevity genes" were believed to be inherited. By examining the DNA of closely related centenarians, the study had already helped to single out certain "genetic signatures" that characterized human longevity.

To most, the series of letters representing the four components on a DNA molecule—A, C, G and T—looked no more illuminating than alphabet soup, an indecipherable string of letters. But the cryptic pathways of centenarian siblings held within them a potential cure for aging, and the diseases that went along with aging, such as Alzheimer's disease, stroke, cancer and heart disease.

It had been proven that many centenarians did indeed *have* genes for such diseases in their DNA. But their study had helped to show that even if an elderly person did end up developing a disease, hardly any of the elderly that ended up living past one hundred actually died from it, leading many researchers to believe that the presence of the "longevity genes" helped to protect them from the diseases.

More interesting to Ryan was the fact that the findings pointed toward huge developments in the fields of personal genomics and predictive medicine, a potential gold mine for the likes of him. He was convinced that someday soon the scalpel would be replaced by the use of therapeutic cells and proteins; life spans would be considerably enhanced by the careful manipulation of genes that actually *change the DNA*, make it more able to resist disease and aging; doctors would be able to match drugs with patients and prescribe supplements, nutraceuticals, and pharmaceuticals that would stop the cells from dying and preserve the functioning parts of the body that normally decline with age.

Ryan knew that the baby boomers would pay top dollar for such life-enhancing drugs, and he planned to be at the center of it all. Perhaps he'd be rich and famous one day!

Yet, in spite of all of the ground-breaking developments, the field of genetics, in relation to longevity, was still very much a mystery, similar to the reaches of outer space. Researchers still couldn't pinpoint all of the longevity genes involved, nor their exact function in lifespan extension. It was like identifying a planet in a faraway galaxy, but not knowing its relationship to the galaxy in which it was placed. There was still so much to understand, in order to truly change the course of humanity.

For his part, Ryan still clung stubbornly to the belief that the only way to move the world's understanding of longevity forward was by studying the world's supply of biologically related elderly. He firmly believed that the powerful genetic pathways of biologically related centenarians held within them a potential cure for aging, and the diseases that went along with aging. They also, for Ryan and a growing number of other researchers, harbored the secret to *defeating death itself.*

Even though some gerontologists—doctors specializing in the medical needs of the elderly—believed that the maximal duration of human life was already programmed at 110 to 115 years and would never change, Ryan believed without a doubt that a combination of genetics and biochemistry would soon prove them wrong.

∞

Rose lounged on Ryan's bed, watching him shove textbooks into his backpack. In addition to his part-time research associate job, he was also a Ph.D. student in a prestigious biochemistry and molecular genetics program. He hardly had time for a full eight hours of sleep, but he managed it, mostly by restricting his free time pursuits.

"I hope you left enough room in there for this," she said, flipping the pages of the western Ireland tour book.

"I already read it," he said. "There's not much to read about an island that's only three miles long and two miles wide."

She eyed him critically. "Are you sure you're...okay to travel?"

"Of course!" Ryan huffed. Just because he had been a bit tired last month and had passed out in the lab and was rushed to the emergency room and had stayed in the hospital for a full week for heart palpitations, chest tightness and inexplicable sweating didn't warrant such a big fuss, in his opinion.

"My dad wanted me to remind you to bring the journal he bought you. And the yoga mat."

"Your dad is a worry wart," Ryan laughed. "Tell him I won't have time for sedentary aerobics."

"Ireland is beautiful," Rose said wistfully. "I wish I could go with you."

"I don't care about sightseeing," he scoffed, zipping his backpack with great effort. In addition to his books, he'd packed his noise reduction earphones and laptop.

"What is it with you?" she asked, her roundly innocent face unusually serious.

He shrugged as he dumped his vitamins and supplements into a plastic bag and molded it into the corner of his suitcase.

Rose lifted the bottom corner of Ryan's tidy, tan comforter to peer at the sheets. "Hospital corners," she scolded. "I knew it."

"My work is important to me," he said. "The Okinawans, the Sardinians of Italy, the Seventh-Day Adventists in California, the Costa Ricans on the Nicoya Peninsula, perhaps these Irish women I'm going to meet. They all carry genetic gold, you know, and mining this gold takes time, effort. Milling about the Irish coastline is not on the agenda."

"You're only twenty-eight years old," said Rose. "Live a little."

Ryan snorted. *Live a* lot, he wanted to say. *That's what* I'm *trying to do*.

2

———

The giggling toddler in a polka-dotted face mask peeked over the top of the airplane seat at Ryan.

"Hi," Ryan said reluctantly, looking up from his molecular genetics textbook and half-way removing his earphones, which at that moment were piping the crescendo of Chopin's Nocturne in C Minor into his ear.

"What's your name?" he asked. His voice from behind the N95 face mask sounded a little like Darth Vader's.

The child's brown eyes rounded, and he squealed. He turned to his mother. "Mammy!" he said in a thick Irish accent. "That man is mad!"

"Oh, no, he's not," the mother cooed. "Not mad, love."

He heard the boy's mother kiss the child on the cheek, a dry smacking.

"No, mammy. Not mad. *Sad,*" he corrected. "He's a sad man."

The mother shushed him and opened a bag of snacks for him.

Ryan closed the book abruptly and leaned his head back, resting his neck. He took a couple of deep breaths, but filling his lungs with stale air, filtered through his mask, made his belly turn. He massaged his chest, which never seemed to loosen. Sometimes the pectoral muscles were so tight he believed he was having a heart attack.

Ryan glanced at the closed door of the cockpit. He tried not to imagine the pilots inside, chatting with one another and pushing levers and buttons. His father had been an airplane pilot, but he had died, ironically, in a car accident when Ryan was only six. His brother Daniel, three years old at the time, had been killed in the accident as well. He and his mother had been left with the wreckage.

Perhaps he *was* sad.

He gritted his teeth and pulled down the window shade. The limitless black sky beyond made him want to hug himself out of loneliness and fear, and the intense proximity of strangers heightened the sensation.

The young woman in the seat next to him wore a white v-neck t-shirt that showcased a golden chain, just dipping into the convex lines of cleavage; she'd seemed interested in his eyeglasses and had given Ryan quite an eyeful in her effort to examine them.

In responding to her polite queries regarding occupation and education, he'd been reminded of the complexity of male-female interactions, and he'd retreated within his books and notes. For the last two hours, she hadn't uttered a word, preferring instead to watch an inane romantic comedy (as if there were any other kind of romance) on the screen above them.

He maintained a careful distance between his body and hers, even as he reached into his backpack and pulled out a banana. He wasn't hungry for food, but he removed his mask and ate it anyway, mentally adding 108 calories to his total for the day.

Now the peel sat lifelessly on his pull-down tray, its yellow skin turning to brown right before his eyes.

∞

A few months ago, Ryan had flown with Dr. Buxton to Okinawa, a series of small islands southwest of mainland Japan. Okinawa, with incredibly reliable age-verification records, boasted the largest concentration of centenarians in the world and one of the world's longest average life expectancies. Intriguing to Ryan's particular research study was the fact that the centenarians had many close elderly relatives living nearby.

Dr. Buxton and Ryan spent two months there, working with a couple of scientists of similar research studies to compare and collect data. Ryan single-handedly collected dozens of cheek swabs from related elderly Okinawans—local celebrities—with small, specialized Q-tips, which he rubbed over the inner cheek's surface. He designed several family trees as he went through the island, double-checking names and dates.

But Dr. Buxton, a gerontologist by trade, had been more concerned with interacting with the people, young and old alike, and chose to conduct two-hour interviews with an interpreter. He was fascinated with the centenarians' lifestyles: the centenarians still worked or remained physically active, ate mostly vegetables, fish, tofu and seaweed, and were active in their families and in their communities, which took pride in their advanced ages.

The beefy Dr. Buxton, with his scruffy beard and aviator sunglasses, walked along the white-sand beaches, gathering exotic flowers and snapping photographs of the blue sea to show Ryan upon his return. He took karate lessons from a ninety-five-year-old master. He worked in the garden of a 104-year-old woman, who still babysat her six great-grandchildren every day.

But Ryan had seen through these outward manifestations, clear to the DNA in the centenarians' cells. Some of his findings were published in a paper, and several major pharmaceutical companies had begun to take an interest in their particular longevity study.

Dr. Buxton had then reminded him that the Okinawan *lifestyle* provided many reasons why they were so healthy so far into their senior years. Genetics, after all, only accounted for twenty-five percent of human longevity. It was lifestyle that really mattered, and Ryan knew all about that.

He noted the influx of Kentucky Fried Chicken and McDonald's restaurants on the island, and the growing rate of obesity in the younger generations. Disconcertingly, the life spans of modern-day Okinawans now almost matched the average life spans in Japan.

Ryan had been satisfied with the Okinawan progress and had begun to add more eastern items to his limited diet, including bitter melon and seaweed. But the glory of the project had soon faded; he needed more, and different, DNA samples to further his work.

Ideally, Ryan needed a genetically homogenous population

of people from a small gene pool. *Like elderly people on an island off the western coast of Ireland*, he thought.

∞

The ferry to the island was delayed, said the toothless barman who tended the dark pub at the harbor. No explanation was offered, even though the big, red-hulled boat rocked tenderly in the placid water.

It had been surprisingly sunny in the sleepy coastal village when Ryan had placed his rolling suitcase in the rental's trunk. He had been expecting buckets of rain, Ireland-style, but the proprietor of the hotel told him that the coast was experiencing a rare dry spell, with warm weather to boot.

He was glad that he had remembered to bring along his favorite sunscreen, SPF 90. He still smelled it on his palms, even though he was sure he had washed it all off.

"You might as well have a pint," the barman said, already filling a smudged glass at the tap.

It was only 10:30 in the morning, but Ryan pretended to be thankful, cupping his hands around the warmish glass of beer. The truth was that he had no taste for beer. The beverage boasted its barley and hops, but it was basically empty calories. The only alcoholic drink that suited him was red wine, for the heart-healthy benefits of the resveratrol.

Two stools over, a bald man in a grey suit with frayed cuffs watched him from under his eyelids. Ryan took a small sip of the thick, brown liquid.

"Goin' to the island," said the man in a dense Irish accent. "Not much there but rocks and gulls."

"I'm not staying long. Just four nights," said Ryan, taking another sip of beer. It wasn't that bad, really.

"More gulls than people out there, now." The man paused to drink half the glass of beer in one practiced swallow. "You one for the feathers?"

"No," Ryan admitted. "I don't like birds."

The man's bloodshot eyes bulged. "Don't like birds? That's a pity."

Ryan sipped his beer, amazed to see only a bit of backwash in the bottom of the glass. Without asking, the barman grabbed his glass and filled it at the tap again.

The clock on the wall ticked slowly as Ryan started on the second beer, another pint of approximately 200 calories. His stomach bulged, as if he'd eaten an entire meal, and his head felt as if it were stuffed with straw, his body rubbery and disconnected.

"So what are you up to out there if you aren't a hiker?" the man asked.

Ryan thought it wouldn't hurt to tell him. "I'm a research associate for a study, back in the States. We've heard of some extremely elderly women on the island, and I've come to check it out. See what we can learn."

The man nodded. "Plenty of old on the island. That's all that's left. Young people won't stay on, and the old just get older."

The barman glanced out the bright window. "If it isn't the men now."

Ryan craned his neck toward the window and saw a man with wild, white hair walking on the front deck of the ferry. He was accompanied by two younger mates, who were depositing bulging, burlap sacks on the decks. They all wore bright orange oilskins and black Wellingtons, despite the fine weather.

"Is that the captain?" Ryan asked the barman.

"Aye, and lookin' a bit light on his feet, too. It's the weather, it is. Next you know we'll be munchin' on grass."

"I gather it's quite warm for Ireland in late October," said Ryan, fishing around with ogre's hands in his back pocket. His belly was now a gooey ball of dough. He hoped it would be an easy crossing.

"Quite warm!" the man mocked. "Sure, but it's warmer than July, and altogether more sun than we'll see the whole of winter."

"I guess I should count myself lucky it isn't raining," answered Ryan, placing some euros on the bar.

The man looked doubtful though. "I wouldn't be saying that, now."

Ryan shouldered his backpack and rolled his suitcase to the door. Outside, he took deep pulls of the fresh ocean air and felt his brain disinfect. Across the glistening slate of water, he could just make out a smudge of grey, a few miles off, on the otherwise clear horizon.

∞

From the bench on the back of the ferry, he watched the island from a sideways position as it slowly grew to reality. Greenish brown, sometimes glimmering gold in the light of the sun, it was a mountainous rock in the ocean, abandoned in the volcanic shift of the continents.

Beside him, the ferry churned the water, blue as a doll's eye underneath the foam. Clouds like moth wings traced the sky.

Closer, he saw white and gray buildings on the angular hills of the island, and beige sheep scattered here and there among the mossy rocks. White sand beaches, bordered with boulders of gray, circled the island on one side. A squat lighthouse sat upon some giant rocks at the mouth of the harbor.

About thirty minutes later, the ferry moored in the bay. One of the mates helped Ryan into a punt and rowed him to the docks, where a few small motorized fishing boats were anchored. He clambered up to the docks, and the mate handed him his suitcase and pointed out the inn, a two-story stone building.

Ryan planned to check in and ask directions to the sisters' houses. He would go there immediately and interview Cleona, and perhaps her sister Catherine afterward. He would get cheek swabs from them, ask for various sources of age documentation. Then, after taking swabs from the other elderly islanders and their close relatives, he would leave them to crack open the books. He already felt he was falling behind.

Theodore, his thesis adviser, had questioned the five-day furlough, even though the explanation was connected to his program of study. Just thinking of Theo's dubious expression caused Ryan's chest to contract. He walked faster down the pier, but once his feet found the ivory sand of the beach, he slowed, taking a few tentative steps through the softness. He bent down and raked his fingers through it, the way Dr. Buxton would have done in Okinawa.

Further down the shore, the canoe-shaped hulls of discarded boats lay scattered over the pristine shore. Herring gulls perched atop them, watching the water. There were no trees on the island. It had been carved clean, and now stood vulnerable to every whim of nature. There was a deep silence, a feeling of freedom.

He had read in his travel book that the island was part of the "Celtic fringe," the most westerly part of Europe where Celtic traditions and language still held sway; Ireland, Scotland, Wales, Cornwall, Brittany and Isle of Man still paid homage to a Celtic tradition that existed well before the Roman Republic expansion.

On a satellite map, Ireland puffed up, lushly green, to the north-west of continental Europe, and was decorated by hundreds of small islands and islets in the dark blue water. Great Britain, another island, loomed across the Irish Sea to the east.

Ryan had read that some of the smaller islands around Ireland had been abandoned in the last two centuries, not able to keep pace with the march of the modern world.

He could easily see why such islands had missed the world's scramble to industrialism—they were more a part of the Atlantic than of the hulking land mass of Europe.

3

———————

Ryan had been to Europe two years ago, spending a week in France while interviewing three elderly siblings.

The two sisters and brother, aged 99, 101, and 103, had also claimed that their entire village, nestled in the Pyrenees, had a history of longevity. They believed that the longevity was due to the clear mountain air and goat's milk, but their younger relatives had contacted the study for a more scientific explanation.

Ryan had badly wanted to investigate, for no research had yet been done on the village or its centenarians. Ryan had also always felt a vague pulling toward Europe—as if something important were there, waiting for him—so he'd convinced Dr. Buxton to send him there to take DNA samples. After all, France was a known hotbed of longevity. It boasted many healthy and happy centenarians, as well as super-centenarians, and their genes and lifestyles were constantly being studied.

France had also produced history's oldest woman in the world, Jeanne Calment. Not only did Madame Calment live to the well-verified age of 122, but her brother lived to the age of ninety-seven, her father to the age of ninety-three, and her mother to the age of eighty-six. Ryan had guessed that the family genes must have been strong enough to protect their bodies from the effects of smoking and a diet rich in olive oil, port wine and chocolate.

But after sunny days and grassy picnics, he'd come away from the French village in disappointment.

During a visit to the municipality's records basement, he had been able to establish the siblings' family history going back four generations—all of them had lived their lives in the same village.

The two sisters and brother had then taken him to a graveyard and showed him the family plot, pointing out dates of birth and death for him. Ryan had been excited to find two other centenarians on their family tree, one of whom was born in the late seventeenth century. He had also spoken with the other elderly in the area, who remembered the siblings when they were growing up. The villagers seemed to think they were all of similar age.

Ryan had believed, in a rush of excitement, that he'd discovered another "Blue Zone" similar to Okinawa and Sardinia and the Nicoya Peninsula in Costa Rica, where centenarians abounded. The mountainous area was mostly isolated from outside influences, allowing the people to maintain traditional social values and simplified diet that fostered longevity.

Yet just by checking the municipal registers, he'd discovered that other than the siblings who'd originally contacted the study, the elderly in the village had inflated their ages, in some cases by as much as twenty years, and had offered him little official documentation, such as birth certificates, marriage certificates and baptismal records. He would have welcomed even a military certificate or an old passport, but all he was offered was a family Bible, written in French.

This wasn't uncommon in the field of investigative gerontology; Dr. Buxton said the history of longevity was a book of myths, prolonged by the inaccurate or nonexistent birth and death records clear through the late nineteenth century, for most countries. People took pride in a loved one's longevity, which invariably led to jumped conclusions.

However, back in the laboratory, he'd been excited to find variations in the siblings' FOX03A genes—a key gene that associated with extreme longevity. Yet further studies were still needed to pinpoint just exactly how these special genes extended lifespan. He had banked the DNA samples and focused on the future.

He was aware of the fact that as the baby boomers aged, he would have many more samples to analyze. He knew that centenarians were the fastest-growing demographic group in many developed nations, including the U.S., Japan and many countries in Western Europe.

The increase was attributed to the dramatic decrease in childhood-related mortality at the turn of the century, with the advent of vaccines, safe water supplies and better public health in general. There was also better health care for middle-aged and older people in the areas of prevention, screening and interventions in diseases like stroke and cardiovascular disease.

Simply put, people weren't dying as much.

The research study in which he was involved was just one of a number of centenarian studies, with varying emphases, that had emerged in the last twenty years or so. They collaborated, in most cases, to further the study of genetics and longevity. Dr. Buxton was always more than happy to share the study's latest results, to discuss roadblocks and misunderstandings, to compare samples.

Yet, after years of research, Ryan's need for personal success had grown. As much as he liked Dr. Buxton, he didn't consider him a true geneticist. Ryan knew that he would eventually strike out on his own, perhaps as early as his Ph.D. degree was conferred. Such isolation and focus was necessary, he told himself, for the benefit of humanity.

Didn't everyone want to live forever?

∞

As he neared the hotel, Ryan passed a substantial vegetable garden and several rusty bikes propped in a stand. A battered tour bus was parked on the grass in the back. Near the front entrance were a few picnic tables, where a rotund, blonde man in sunglasses sat writing in a notebook. He didn't look up when Ryan wheeled his suitcase loudly by.

At the hotel's cramped reception area, he waited at least fifteen minutes for someone to appear. A glaze of cooking grease coated the air. He heard two women behind a door, speaking rapidly in Gaelic. It seemed as if the conversation, hitting notes both high and low, would never stop. After a long while, a middle-aged woman with gray, wiry hair and an ample bosom emerged from the door.

"Oh dear, I do hope you haven't been standin' there too long!" she exclaimed, wiping her hands on a threadbare apron.

"Not too long," he said. He wondered what would be considered "too long" on this island.

"I don't have many folks stayin' on this time of year, and I'm gettin' altogether used to it," she said, bustling about the desk, lifting papers and books in a harried rush.

"I'm Ryan Abernathy. Staying until Sunday?"

"Oh, aye," she said, consulting a big, open book on the desk with a calloused forefinger. "Here you are."

She rustled some more papers, then opened a drawer in the desk and presented him with a big, old-fashioned key. "Room 10. It's the best one I have. Renovated just last year. Brand new bed linens and curtains, you know."

"Great," he said. "What is your Wi-Fi code?"

She looked embarrassed. "I'm afraid we don't have it here. You'll have to go to the library or the community center down the road if you're wantin' the internet."

Ryan wondered how a business could operate without immediate internet access. He recalled that he'd had to leave a phone message when he'd made his reservation. It had been this woman—he remembered that her name was Dorothy Sullivan—who had called him back to confirm; he still recalled her melodic flow of words, so different from the staccato version of the language spoken in America.

She gestured to the flowered wallpaper, the pale pink woodwork, the nautical decorations.

"You'll be sure to get some rest and relaxation here, so. Nice and warm too for your holiday. Americans are sun-worshippers, so they are. I don't even recognize me four children anymore. They all live in the States now, so, and gettin' a tan is their favorite thing in the world."

He looked down at his white hands and smiled. "I'm not

here for a holiday. I'm here to visit a couple of elderly women on the island. The Owens? Perhaps you know them."

Her upturned face slumped into befuddlement. "Aye."

Ryan experienced the often-felt feeling that he'd said something he shouldn't have.

"If you could give me some directions to their houses, I'd greatly appreciate it," he continued.

Lips pursed, she slid a piece of paper from a drawer and hastily drew a map.

"They live next door to each other, on the very far edge of the island," she said, her voice disapproving. "But good luck to you gettin' the old girls to the door. Whatever business it is you're doin' with 'em, it won't be enough to get 'em out of their beds."

"I'd heard they weren't well," he offered.

"Aye, both are mighty old, but you must already know that," she said, her eyes narrowing. "You're not from Hollywood, now, are you?"

He laughed a bit. "No, sorry."

She exhaled loudly in relief. "We had a Hollywood director stay on last year," she explained. "Wanted to make a film, you know, with parts of it set on an island off the west coast of Ireland. Him and his fancy people had us scurrying round like rabbits, trying to please 'em."

"What happened?"

"Oh, they decided on an abandoned island, said it was easier to film there altogether."

"That's too bad," he said. "Could have been great for business, I imagine."

"Aye," she sighed sadly. "But then, we would have been

swarmed to death with even more of the foreigners, and I don't think this island could have taken it."

Ryan agreed. He'd read that there was only one hotel and one pub on the island.

"Thanks for the map," he said, reaching down to grab the handle of his suitcase.

He felt her eyes on his back as he maneuvered his suitcase up the carpeted flight of stairs.

∞

After a quick face-wash and readying of his backpack, he returned to the reception area, where he poured himself a cup of lukewarm tea. The alcohol in the beer had incited a desperate thirst. Dorothy was now seated behind the desk, speaking with the man who'd been writing at the picnic table.

"Oh, the West Village is inhabited. Just barely so," he heard Dorothy say. "But it's probably not the best choice of a writing spot."

"Why is that?" the man asked in a British accent.

"Well...it's a bit worn down, I'd say. Vacant, really. I myself haven't set a foot over there in a good twenty years. There's not at thing there a-tall."

The writer consulted a brochure in his hand. "I was hoping to get a view of the cliffs. And the remains of that old church. They're quite popular, according to the literature."

"I'd try the beaches first," she said firmly. Dorothy looked curiously at his notebook. "What are you writing at, anyway?"

He shrugged. "I'm not sure yet. I'm looking for ideas."

"Are you a *real* writer?"

He laughed. "I'm a published poet."

"We get all kinds of artists and writers out here," she said. "It's inspirational, so they say."

"Oh, I'm sure I'll meet the muse out here," he said. "The island has a certain truth to it. Godly purity."

She snorted. "I'm not from here originally—my husband, God rest his soul, was born and bred here—and we ran the hotel together after we married. I've endured this island, but isn't not an easy thing. The first time I heard that wind comin' off the sea, I knew why it was said to be the calling of the dead," she said with a knowing nod. "The voices of the drowned seamen, calling out their names on a dark, rainy night. It's enough to make you walk on water back to Ireland."

"If I'm not mistaken, this *is* Ireland," said the writer good-naturedly.

She smiled at him in pity. "No, it isn't, love. It isn't a-tall."

∞

Ryan slipped past them out the front door, map in hand. He found the main road, lined harshly in black by Dorothy, that seemed to cut across the entire length of the island. As he wound up and down the hills, he felt more like himself, as his legs stretched in front of him, igniting his mind and warming his blood.

He was no writer, but he too had acknowledged the island's appeal. He couldn't escape the feeling that he'd been dropped on the edge of the world, that he now lumbered down a road not into the future, but a pathway into the past. It was hard to rectify the island with what he'd read recently of the new high-tech, fast-track Ireland of the European Union.

The landscape was fairly hilly; across the sloping green meandered low stone walls, an attempt to mark territory. He heard the ocean all about him. The calling of the birds and the sloped necks of the sheep and cows in the rocky grazing area put him in mind of a cold-weather paradise.

But the naked daylight revealed the island's less-than-pure reality.

The pot-holed road was dotted here and there with loads of manure. Trash was strewn here and there along the road: rusty tin cans, cracked plastic buckets, old bottles, broken crab pots, candy wrappers. A handful of cars were parked randomly across the fields, no rhyme or reason for their final destinations. The walls and fences that appeared so pastoral from afar now appeared crumbled, misshapen; the slumped wood of the fences was strung with wire and even string.

The farther he walked, the more desolate the terrain became. According to the map, he guessed he'd arrived in the West Village, but it wasn't much of a village at all. The houses, huddled into a slope of hill, were mostly identical rectangles of concrete or stone. A few were now empty stone shells, their wood and roofs stripped and nettles growing where the floors used to be—eerie reminders of lives once lived, families once raised. The withered fields about him were covered in black birds with white chests, picking their way across the land with business-like precision.

Despite the sunshine and a building excitement, depression gnawed within him.

The lonely West Village, at the end of the road and the edge of the island, was very different from the East, where the tourists' money showed itself in the freshly painted pastel shutters and lace half-curtains in the two-story windows. Out here, there were no children, no clotheslines, and too much space between houses. The village seemed broken, in mourning, and yet it shared its life with the ever-changing Atlantic, with nothing but the seabirds to share the views with.

The inhabitants of the abandoned houses must have watched the ships chug by, maybe even airplanes puff across the sky. Looking at a grassy space where once there had been a table and chairs and perhaps a bed, he wondered what the stones had overheard on the family's final day on the island, if there were plans of return uttered, hope for a more exciting life elsewhere.

The seabirds soared above the ruins; like the stones, they too seemed to know things he could never fathom. They flew around and around, just out of reach, watching him, watching the sea.

4

____

Aisling ambled down the road that ran from one side of the island to the other. Ever since her best friend Kiley had left the island seven years ago, she walked the high road every day.

It felt good to walk across the island that seemed to grow smaller and smaller as she grew older. She enjoyed the stretching of the muscles in her thighs, the pull of her calves. She inhaled deeply of the fresh air, feeling the expansion in her middle like a belly full of warm bread.

Her rubber boots squeaked dully on the pebbles underfoot, and strands of her ropy red hair brushed across her face. She saw the local grammar school teacher, Miss MacGinley, making her way to the little store, stocked mostly with canned goods and boxes of instant potatoes and muffin mix. Aisling wondered how long the new teacher would last on the island, if she'd leave within one or two years like the rest of the unmarried, mainland imports, dissatisfied with the challenge that only seven children offered.

When she reached the East Village, Aisling stopped to rest on the beach that softened that part of the island. She gazed out, far out across the water to where the mainland lay. She caught sight of the ferry churning back to the mainland, and of course she thought of Kiley and wondered if she was happy in her nanny position in Dublin.

Aisling went to the mainland for shopping excursions, to sell her hand-knit sweaters and to pick up things not available on the island, but her experience had been limited to one small coastal village much like the island. The people there tended to stare at her, so she disliked going.

It boggled her mind to imagine the hundreds of thousands of people in the bigger cities of the world, people of all races and religions, living their lives together. The thought of touching the hands of strangers in hundreds of small exchanges, breathing the air that had once circulated in an unknown human's chest, both exhilarated and terrified her.

She leaned back into the sand to watch the terns that circled the shore, ceaselessly searching. She wished that she too could lift up from the ground and hover above the island, to see what it looked like from the sky.

On bad days, when she was tired and run down from work, with no one to confide in, she entertained the notion of flying away from the island. She sometimes went west, over the gray wool of the sky toward a life of opportunity in America, but sometimes she went east, crossing Ireland and Great Britain and even Europe. But in the end, she always came back to the island, lonely and disappointed with what she'd found. To Aisling, it seemed easier just to stay put.

She grew warm in the wool sweater, sitting in the unusually

strong sun, but she felt too lazy to remove it. She didn't mind an occasional spell of warmth as long as the southwest brought the cooling rain clouds, the rainbows of change. The recent prolonged warm spell was a bad omen.

She stood up, brushed the sand off the seat of her jeans and began the walk back to the West Village, where she lived with her *Mamo* in a small cottage that hunkered into a furze-covered hill near the cliffs that dropped straight down, 350 feet, to the beating Atlantic.

Tourists came to the island primarily to marvel at the brutally striated cliffs and the rubble of the old West Village church. Bearing small, silver cameras and strange accents, the summer tourists swarmed the island's hotel, pub and community center. They biked, hiked, snorkeled and swam all over the island, as good as land owners in their possessiveness.

Aisling waited for October, when the weather on the island turned colder and more stormy and the tourists practically ran for the ferry back to the mainland. Most of the other islanders, however, were somewhat saddened, for they had grown accustomed to the tourists, to the infusion of energy and news of the world. Over the last fifty years, tourism had become the island's primary source of income, since the island was easier to reach with the faster, more regular ferry service. English was now spoken on the island, even more than the Irish dialect that had been used for as long as anyone knew. And English was taught in the primary school, where Aisling had attended until the age of twelve.

Most of the eighty or so islanders were well over the age of sixty; the young people chose to make a living in Scotland and Ireland and the United States (still "the new land" to her *Mamo*).

Once gone, the islanders hardly ever returned.

∞

Kiley hadn't waved when the ferry departed the island that dreary day. Watching the boat strain through the water, Aisling had felt the strange desire to leave the island too, to never come back, and it had filled her with sadness.

Afterward, Aisling began to have a recurring dream in which she was a corncrake, the island's secretive and endangered meadow-nester. She sat upon an empty nest; she was alone in the black meadow, and the mower's blades rumbled toward her. She had nowhere to turn. She always awoke, sweaty and gasping, and hoping that her cries hadn't woken her *Mamo*.

Lost in thoughts of the dream, Aisling almost didn't register the man, standing with a hand on the wooden gate outside her cottage.

He was a tourist, obviously, with his bright blue pack and clean, light brown pants and too-white shirt. Most of the islanders wore drably colored, outdated hand-me-downs, topped with oilskins.

"You've lost the way to the cliffs. They're further on, northwest," she said, pointing out the direction. "This is a private home."

"Oh, I'm not looking for the cliffs," he said, in what Aisling knew was an American accent. She could also pick out Dutch, German, French and British.

He was a handsome man, with a headful of curly brown hair that framed an expertly carved face. Kind, brown eyes hid behind his speckled glasses. He was tall and thin, perhaps even skinny.

"I'm trying to find Cleona Owen." He consulted a hand-drawn map. "Is this her cottage?"

She bit her lip hard, and heard herself ask, "What are you wantin' with Cleona?"

He smiled, surprising her with his perfect, white teeth, another anomaly on the island. "I'm here to inquire of her age, which I've heard to be over one hundred years old, and to possibly interview her for a study of centenarians I'm involved in. I've heard that she's not alone, either."

"Alone?" she asked.

"I heard that she has an elderly twin sister. Catherine."

Aisling grew aware of how uncomfortably hot she'd become during the walk; her chest rose and fell as if she'd been running. She swayed, as she wiped her damp brow with the sleeve of her sweater. Her eyes closed.

"Are you alright?" he asked, suddenly close. She opened her eyes and flinched to see his face only inches from hers. She noticed a shadow of stubble covering his strong jaws.

Before she could muster an answer, he touched her forehead firmly with his palm—strangely soft, unlike the hands of Murray that scraped her skin almost painfully when he only tried to caress.

"You seem warm...perhaps overheated. It could be the sweater."

She watched him unzip his pack and rummage around, pulling out a half-empty plastic bottle of water. She didn't think she was thirsty, but she drank the warm water greedily, felt it puddle into her belly.

"We're not used to this kind of weather so late in October. It was bitter cold and storming not five days ago," she said, licking her chapped lips.

"Your face is still as white as a sheet. Let me help you home."

She rubbed her cheeks with both hands, thinking. She finally said, "I live here. Cleona's my great-grandmother."

"Oh!" he exclaimed. "It's you!"

"Me?"

"I was told that she lived with her great-granddaughter. I would have called, you know, but I was told you don't have a telephone. Or a computer. I would have e-mailed." He grinned brightly. "My name is Ryan Abernathy."

After a moment, she remembered herself. "I'm Aisling."

She pushed open the blue gate with hands that seemed large and dreamlike. "How did you find us?"

"A Dr. Fitzgerald called the study. He said he paid a visit to your great-grandmother and her sister a week ago." He added apologetically, "He said they were ill, but he thought our research study would be interested in their DNA. I came as quickly as I could."

"DNA," she repeated. Conversing in English—a second language to her—wasn't usually this difficult.

"Their genetic codes. Long-lived relatives are very important to us. Especially twins."

Aisling's head lurched again. She knew she shouldn't have called the doctor; he had turned out to be entirely too curious, despite his goodwill. But the traditional herbs had failed to help, and Aisling's worry had won over her caution.

And yet, despite the blue "antibiotic" pills that the doctor had insisted she take, *Mamo* was still dying, and Catherine hadn't risen from her bed.

Aisling led him to the open door of the cottage, as if she'd done that kind of thing her entire life. In spite of the heat, she shivered, almost feverish.

"She sleeps most of the day," she said. "Would you care for a cup of tea until she wakes?"

"I could come back later, when she's feeling up to it," he offered.

"Please," she found herself say. "Do stay for a cup."

"Well, one cup, if it's no trouble."

She stepped inside the cottage, leaving the door open. Despite the heat outside, it was still cool in the low, stone house. She took one brief look at him as he stepped inside, to prove to herself that this man was indeed standing in her cottage. Then she poured some water into the kettle for tea and sliced some freshly baked brown bread.

Ryan seated himself at the table and removed his pack. He looked curiously about the cottage, at the oil lamps, the white-washed walls, the earthen floor, the soot-stained hearth.

"I suppose you're wondering on our old-fashioned ways, coming from America like you are," she said.

"A little, yes," he admitted.

"We like it this way," she said, thinking that it was really Cleona who'd insisted that nothing change from her girlhood. "We wouldn't know what to do with all the amenities. Cleona even balked at a gas stove, but I won her over, in the end. We still have the pot-oven though."

She pointed to the ceiling. "A hundred years ago, the cottage used to be thatched with rushes, but now it's tarred felt."

She couldn't stop herself from talking.

His eyes continued to dance around the room. "Well, your

home is charming. In America, it's McMansions everywhere you look."

"What's a McMansion? It isn't a crack on the Irish, I hope?"

"Oh no," he said quickly. "I think the term derived from McDonald's, maybe. You know, the super-sized meals."

Aisling stared, unsure how to answer him. *Who was McDonald?*

"Well, a McMansion is not the nicest term for an overly large one-family home," he said.

"One-family?"

"This cottage is a more economical use of space, is what I'm trying to say."

"I've heard everything in America is big," she offered, as she fetched two cracked blue plates from the cupboard. "Big and tall and new."

"That's about right."

"It's different here."

"So I've seen," he said. He sounded as if a laugh was in his throat.

"The hotel has running water and electricity," he said, looking about.

"We all do. It was thirty years ago, when the Irish government thought to step up and help us. The improvements, so they call them, have made people even lazier than they were. Won't even get out of bed before noon, and when they do, they're glued to the television."

"What are the buckets of water for?"

"That pipe water is full of the chlorine. It rots the teeth and does who knows what devilry to your insides. I fetch water from a spring nearby."

"Every day?"

She pointed to the buckets of fresh water that they used for drinking and cooking. Then she pointed to the empty fixture on the beam of the ceiling. "We've never even put in a bulb. And the winds knock the lines down half the year anyways. It's all useless."

He continued to stare around him, and Aisling poured steaming water from the kettle into two cups with a shaking hand. She couldn't keep up with this man, this bright-eyed American with the inquisitive mind.

As he reached down to rummage in his pack, Aisling poured the black tea into the waste bucket. She measured two shots of poteen—Murray's illegally distilled Irish whiskey— into the wooden barrel cups, then plunked them down on the table.

"Who needs tea on such a fine day as this?" she declared, picking up a barrel. "*Sláinte*," she said, raising the barrel in the air.

Ryan shifted in his chair. He sniffed the barrel. She saw, beneath his curls, his forehead wrinkle.

"It's just a drop of drink."

He sighed. "I suppose one drink couldn't hurt." He raised his barrel toward her and said, "*Sláinte.*"

The poteen burned its way into her stomach, but she welcomed the medicinal feeling.

"Are you Irish, then?" she asked.

"Pardon me?"

"Abernathy. That's a Scots-Irish name. From the river Nethy in Scotland."

His eyes grew round behind the glasses. "I didn't know that.

My family…we didn't discuss our ancestry very much. I guess it wasn't that important."

"Not important," she murmured, and blinked in amazement at him, for she couldn't imagine not knowing every detail of her family's background. Even the most distant of relatives seemed like old friends to her. She reached a hand out to pat him gently on his arm; he stared at it as if trying to figure out what it was.

"So what does Owen mean?" he asked, moving his arm away.

"The origins are Latin, meanin' 'good offspring.'"

She poured more poteen into their barrels and tipped its contents into her mouth. But Ryan's eyes leaked drops from their corners. He fingered the barrel gingerly, but didn't pick it up.

"Come now!" said Aisling. "Don't be a mollycoddle."

He laughed, and shook his head. "I'm not used to drinking whiskey during the day. It's filled with calories, you know."

"What the devil are those?" she asked, alarmed.

"Units of energy found in food."

"So calories are good for you, then."

"They are, up to a point," he said. "But you don't want to eat too many of them. It can lead to obesity and all kinds of health problems."

She took note of the bones of his wrist and pushed the platter of freshly baked bread toward him.

"Here. I believe you need a bit of bread, with a good lashing of butter."

He eyed the plate suspiciously. She took a slice, slathered on butter and offered it to him. He nibbled a corner of the crust.

"This bread is amazing," he said, as if surprised.

In spite of her nerves, Aisling smiled at the compliment.

Baking soda, flour, salt and buttermilk from the cow. Watching him chew, she grew hungry for the taste herself. She took a piece from the loaf, and tasted the same saltiness, the warmth.

When he'd finished with the part of the bread that didn't have butter on it, he tipped the rest of the barrel's contents into his mouth.

"You know, I lived with my grandparents for a few years when I was a teenager," he said. Bright pink spots had appeared on his hollowed cheeks. "When my mother died."

Aisling watched his eyes cloud, but said nothing.

"They had a farm and animals too. I know how to milk a cow and saddle a horse," he said proudly. "I didn't like living on the farm at the time, but now...it was simple."

Aisling smiled, still silent. Through the open door, the swirl of the sea could be heard.

"Not many American women would live with their great-grandmothers," he continued. "How old are you? Sixteen, seventeen?"

"I'm 25 years old."

His eyes widened, and he took in her face more closely. She had an urge to drop her head, but she held his gaze.

"Really?" he said. "You look younger. Your skin, I think."

She nodded. "It's in the family."

"Well, women your age are too worried about planning weddings and building careers to care about their aging relatives."

"Where else would I go?" she asked. "What else could I do?"

"It's a big world out there," he said. "Have you ever thought about moving away?"

"No."

"But the island is so small..."

"Aye," she said, and took another slice of bread. She tried hard to keep her mouth closed as she chewed; he watched her so closely now.

"So your great-grandmother and her sister are over one hundred years old," he stated, fingering the handle of the barrel with clean fingers, the nails neatly trimmed at the edges.

"Aye."

He smiled at her. "Are you going to make me guess?"

She shrugged. "I'll tell you, same as I told the doctor. I don't know their exact ages, and I don't believe they do either anymore. Their minds have gone."

The statement, only partly true, was harder to tell to Ryan than it was to the doctor.

"I don't suppose you have any documentation lying around," he said. "A birth certificate or a passport, something with an age or a date on it..."

"No," she said, not meeting his eyes.

"Photographs?" he asked hopefully.

"No, not a one."

After a little more butterless bread and four more barrels of poteen, Ryan's eyes appeared half-closed behind askew glasses, and his skin fell slackly around his mouth.

"I shouldn't have had that last whiskey," he said sleepily. Aisling agreed.

He got up clumsily, almost knocking the chair over as he tried to reach his pack.

"Sit down for a spell, catch your breath there," Aisling said.

He nodded, running a hand through his hair. He slumped onto the chair, causing its legs to pop. Aisling watched in wonder as he fell into a drunken sleep, right before her eyes. After a few moments, his head flopped onto his shoulder.

Aisling gazed at his open-mouthed face for a long time. She wanted to remove his glasses, so that she could she could see his sharp-boned face better, but she didn't want to wake him. Instead, she reached out and touched his hair, so wild on a man so serious and smart. The brownish blonde strands were as soft as the hair on a lamb's ear, as curly as a young lass's.

He slept on, unaware of her scrutiny. She hadn't thought for a moment that the drink would lay the man so flat. She'd only wanted to slow him down for a bit.

She examined his belt, a brown strap that cinched his smooth pants with a silver buckle. She touched the leather gently, at the place where it connected with the cold metal. Unlike his downy hair, the belt was sturdy, serious.

She didn't know what to think of him.

She quietly got up and made her way to the lower room, separated from the kitchen with a cupboard and a dresser. Cleona blinked at her from the wooden bed, her face lifelessly pale. Aisling sat on the edge and began brushing the long white hair.

"All the merry talk brought back memories, but now I can't think what they were," Cleona said in Gaelic. Aisling couldn't believe Cleona had heard the conversation with her bad ears.

"Is the visitor asleep?" she asked.

Aisling smiled. "Aye. He'll doze for a bit."

Cleona cackled softly. "What are you playing at, Orla?"

Aisling ignored the mistake. "He wants to talk to you. About your age."

Cleona began to cough, and Aisling helped raise her up to a

sitting position. The soupy hacking continued. Finally, she said, "Give me my stick."

It was more activity than Cleona had seen in months. Usually Aisling just helped her on and off the chemical toilet and put her back in bed.

Aisling reached down and brought up the walking stick. As she handed it to her, she asked, "Are you up to it?"

"Aye," she breathed. "It's been a long time since we've had a visitor." Her hand trembled on the softly rounded top of the wood.

Aisling held Cleona's upper arm as they made their way slowly through the cottage to where Ryan slumped, a snore wiggling his upper lip.

As they stood over him, there was a sound of heavy footsteps outside the front of the cottage and the squeaking of the gate. Before Aisling could move, Murray crashed over the threshold.

5

A door slammed close by, and a vein deep inside Ryan's head pulsed in pain. His eyelids felt like pockets of lead.

He was in Ireland, he recalled, an island on the edge of the world.

The humble cottage had mesmerized him, as if he had stumbled into a living history exhibit at a museum. He had seen a spinning wheel, of all things.

He smelled burned wood, and his neck burned in an unnatural position.

It occurred to him that he had fallen asleep in the chair, and with a start, he opened his eyes to see an elderly woman sitting in the chair at the table where Aisling had been.

"Oh!" he breathed. He struggled to sit up straight, his vision swimming.

In his confusion, it seemed that the woman was really Aisling covered in Oscar-winning movie makeup. The two women shared almost identical bone structure, skin tone and eyes the color of jade, but where Aisling appeared to be no more than a freshly scrubbed teenager, lithe yet voluptuous and as imposing as a Viking, the elderly woman in front of him appeared positively ancient.

Her skin was pure white, and so thin that it looked like it would fall off the bone if touched too roughly. Age spots bloomed algae-like over her hands and face. Her fingers were as crooked as tree roots, her shoulders were hunched, and he saw, when she smiled kindly at him, that she had no teeth. And yet, her long white hair was still tinged with red.

She wore an intricately knit wool sweater, a floor-grazing skirt and leather slippers on her feet. The woman's heavily lidded, filmy eyes watched him curiously.

He felt his entire body flare in a fight-or-flight response. "Hello," he said, pushing himself to a stand.

"*Dia duit,*" she said, her chest rumbling.

"Are you Cleona Owen?" he asked, struggling to pull a notebook from the backpack.

She put a hand to her ear and shook her head. He spoke the question again, but louder.

"*Tá,*" she said. "*Is é mo ainm Cleona Owen. Agus do ainm?*"

He forced himself to breathe deeply. "Do you speak English, Cleona?"

She shook her head. "*Gaeilge.*"

He didn't know that the woman only spoke Gaelic. He looked around the small room for Aisling, but she was gone. He didn't know why he'd drunk so much whiskey—so much that he'd passed out cold in a stranger's house. He didn't feel that he'd been out for very long, but he had definitely managed to make a fool of himself. Rose and Dr. Buxton wouldn't recognize him now.

"Aisling?" he called.

Through the cottage's open window, he was surprised to see the nearly full moon rising in the indigo sky. He checked his black-banded watch, which read only 5:00 p.m. He heard the cawing of a crow, then the sound of urgent whispering outside.

Cleona pointed a knobby finger toward the open front door.

"One minute," he said, raising up one finger for her.

His entire head ached, and he walked unsteadily to the door on boneless legs. When he stepped outside, he saw Aisling, talking with a tall, rangy man. Aisling's eyes danced at Ryan.

"I must have fallen asleep for a minute," Ryan said to her. "I apologize. It's not something I usually do—drink so much, that is."

The man crossed his arms and grunted. He was gigantic in his black oilskin, with a short, black ponytail at the nape of his neck and dirty rubber boots. He smelled of back-breaking work, of fish and sea. His nose was crooked, the clear result of a bad break, and a vein showed itself across the center of his forehead. Inside the cottage, Ryan heard Cleona's wet cough.

"You should be ashamed of yourself, takin' advantage of a sick, old woman and a helpless girl," he growled.

Ryan placed his palms out, and stammered, "No, no. I didn't want to take *advantage*. I just wanted to meet..."

"I was checkin' up on her, and what do I find? A specky four-eyes tourist passed out in her chair!"

"He's not a tourist," said Aisling. "Like I told you, he's wantin' to talk to Cleona. He's fascinated with her age, so he is."

"None of his business a-tall, is it?"

The man's hands curled into giant fists. It was then that Ryan noticed the dried blood on them. "Away off, Yank. You're done here."

Aisling chewed a thumb nail and didn't look at him. The man reached out and gave him a little shove on his shoulder. Taken aback, Ryan hurried inside to get his backpack. Cleona lifted a gnarled hand at him in farewell. He waved back at her, the way a child would wave bye-bye. He stumbled back out the door.

"I'm so sorry," Ryan said to Aisling.

He couldn't believe it, as he scampered down the dark road. There would be no meeting. No cheek swabs, no family history questionnaires. No dissertation topic, either. And it was a pity, for he was pretty sure that Cleona was one of the oldest people he'd ever met.

∞

With the sun gone, the air was cooler. The stars seemed to cluster directly over the island, and the waxing moon appeared chemically enhanced.

Ryan shook his head in disgust. If all had gone according to plan, he would have watched Aisling root around in an old trunk for the necessary documents, perhaps a couple of black-and-white photographs of the twins. He would have taken out the swabs and showed them to Cleona, demonstrated on his own mouth how to scrape the insides of her cheek. Then he would have gotten their permission to venture next door and repeat the process with Catherine.

If he had skipped the whiskey, he would have missed entirely the angry bouncer at the door. Aisling had offered him *tea* in the beginning, he recalled. *Why in the world did she start pouring endless cups of fire whiskey?*

Now he had nothing to show for the trip to Ireland except a hangover. He thought perhaps that he'd ask Dorothy about serving as an interpreter for Cleona, maybe return tomorrow when things had died down a bit. The man couldn't object to him if he showed up with a local, could he?

He came all the way out here, he told himself. He saw, in the wrinkles on Cleona's face, a map to eternity. He would have to try again.

As he walked, his eyes saw more and more shapes in the dark. To his left were the fields, and in the moonlight, they glowed almost reverently, their earlier, shabbier associations gone for the night. Small lakes twinkled here and there in the hills, and he thought of Aisling, gathering daily buckets of drinking water from a freshwater spring.

It had intrigued him that Aisling shunned such modern conveniences, especially given her caretaking role. In the States, she would be hailed as an innovator in a time of "green" choices. Her photo would appear on the cover of *Time* magazine. The President would hire her to act as a consultant, to describe a more economical, earth-friendly way of living.

But he knew that she hadn't made the choices that she had out of a desire for a greener planet. It was likely all that she had ever known.

As he considered the implications of such an austere life, his foot landed in a soft, sliding pile of manure, invisible in the darkness. Cursing, he hobbled over to the side of the road and stifling an urge to vomit, tried to scrape the bottom of his hiking shoe on a rock. Not sure of his progress, he rubbed the shoe on some weedy grass. Then he continued on his way, peering closely at the moonlit ground the rest of the way back.

He could never live like this, he thought.

As he neared the East Village, the sky grew steadily brighter with electric lights. He passed the pub, a small, concrete building; a glance through the open door brought visions of a handful of older men with hands curled around pints of ale, a babble of high and low tones audible.

Back in his warm hotel room, a tray of cheese, crackers and water rested on his dresser. He quickly poured a glass of water and gulped it down, along with one of his anti-anxiety pills, but he soon noticed a chlorinated aftertaste lingering at the back of his throat. He munched on a cheese and cracker, to rid the flavor from his mouth. Then he added 140 calories for the snack, but decided, mostly out of shame, to just forget about the whiskey and bread that he'd consumed earlier. He vowed to start fresh tomorrow.

Then he removed his books from his pack, spread them out on the bed and bent to his studying. But even the most basic sentences seemed to be written in a foreign language. He decided to turn on the boxy television, but grew frustrated with static on its handful of channels and soon turned it off. He never cared for T.V. anyway.

But now, as the electric light of the lighthouse flashed intermittently through the window, the bizarre events of the last few hours knocked around recklessly in his head. He couldn't escape the forgotten village on the northwestern crest of the island, the handful of south-facing houses huddled into the hills, Aisling living in the debris. He guessed that the winds and the rains buffeted the stones of the cottage more often than not, keeping her and Cleona inside, huddled by a small fire. He imagined spending day after day simply waiting for the rain to stop, and the thought exhausted him.

He rummaged through his suitcase to find his flannel pajamas and his lavender-scented pillowcase, which he stretched over the down-filled pillow. The mattress had a pillow-top on it, but it was too soft for his taste. And it was so warm in the room, despite the open window, that he stripped the bed of its numerous layers of blankets, leaving only a light quilt and the new stiff, white sheets. He didn't need to wear his flannel pajamas, either. He changed into a t-shirt and boxer shorts and plopped down on the bed again.

He was barely asleep when he heard a clunk. Over the lavender on his pillow, he breathed in the sweet scent of turf smoke, clung to cloth. Then he felt the mattress dip down as someone sat on the bed beside him.

"Hey!" he tried to yell, but a rough palm covered his mouth. He shot up as best as he could on the gelatinous mass of pillow top, and not believing his eyes, reached for his glasses on the bedside table.

It was Aisling, her long hair tangled around her shoulders. She still wore the wool sweater.

"Why...what are you doing here?" he whispered, even though his vocal chords thrummed with adrenaline. He remembered that he wore only his boxers, and hastily pulled the quilt over his legs. "How did you get in here?"

"Through the window."

The room was on the second floor, he recalled. His heart still hammering, he peered over at the gaping hole, the curtains barely moving in the warm air. "Do you...do this often?"

"No," she said. He thought he saw a smile stretch the skin of her face. "When I was younger, I'd sneak into the hotel rooms with my friend Kiley. We learned all the nooks in the stones, you know. And where Mrs. O'Sullivan kept the furniture and lamps and all. Seems she's moved things about though."

In the felt of darkness, Ryan struggled with words, for thought. The girl was unstable, he thought, appearing in a victim's room like a blood-sucker in a vampire movie. Even so, it had been a long time since he'd had a woman in his room at night.

"You scared me," said Ryan, regretting the words even before they left his tongue.

"I'm sorry," she said.

"You should be."

"*I'm sorry for what happened today*," she clarified, in a louder voice.

Her pale face loomed in the moonlight flooding the room. Her features were neither masculine nor feminine.

"'Twas botherin' me, you bein' treated that way on the threshold of Cleona's house. Murray was rude, and Cleona was upset by it. She...she wanted to talk to you."

Ryan was silent, but unable to keep from looking at her. "I thought the people of Ireland were known for their hospitality."

"Not in the West Village, they're not," she said. "You're lucky Murray didn't get too angry."

"He seemed pretty angry to me."

"I've seen him blacken men's faces for less. But you're so skinny, he probably worried he'd kill you altogether."

He snorted. Back home, he was proud of his thin stature. Being thin was a sign of self-control, a symbol of good health and prosperity. But here, it seemed more prudent to have some meat on your bones.

"I'll have you know that I'm very fit. I could outrun him, if it came down to it."

Aisling said skeptically, "I wouldn't be so sure. He has a long stride."

"Is he your...boyfriend?"

She took a moment to answer. "Sometimes."

In the silence, he heard the patty-cake slap of the water on the boats in the harbor.

"I have the feeling that you want to keep your grandmother's age a secret. Am I right?" he asked.

She shrugged.

"I research people just like your grandmother, people from all over the world. The elderly people that I've met are proud of their ages, of their history. Their families *want* the publicity. I don't understand why your grandmother's age should be such a secret."

She rose abruptly from the bed and stepped to his open suitcase, set on the bench. To his amazement, she reached into it and pulled out his temporarily useless black rain jacket, still rolled into a ball.

She held it out in front of her. "What kind of fabric is this?"

"Um...nylon, I think."

She peered at the label in the darkness. "You're right. It's nylon."

She shook it and scrunched it. "It's not very heavy, is it?"

"That's the point of the jacket. It's packable."

She sniffed. "Well, you'd want a heavier coat to get along on this island."

He watched in growing embarrassment as Aisling began poking through his toiletry kit. She examined his travel-sized shampoo, toothpaste, floss, deodorant, and peppermint body wash. She unscrewed the bottle of cologne that he had gotten as a free sample once, but had never even opened.

She sniffed. "Is this perfume?"

"It's cologne. For men."

"But you don't wear it," she stated, screwing the top back on.

"How do you know?"

"You smell like lavender," she said. "In the summer, great bunches of lavender grow near the stream where I fetch water."

She moved to the pile of books and papers on the floor by his bed. She picked up one of the heavy books. "I've never seen such a big book. Why did you bring it?"

"I have to study. I'm a doctoral student. It's what we do." Ryan felt his legs begin to sweat beneath the covers.

She read the cover of the *Nuclear Protein Transport* textbook. "I'm not goin' to ask."

She sat down on the bed again, squeezing herself next to his right leg, buried in the quilt. She opened the book to a dog-eared page.

"How old is she, Aisling?"

She slammed the book shut and dropped it to the floor with a loud thump. "It's just a number, age is. It shouldn't have such importance for you. You, with your big books and thin jackets and...McMansions."

"It's important," he said. "To *me*."

She opened her mouth as if to speak, but no sound came out. "I should go, leave you to your sleep," she said. "I only wanted to tell you that I was sorry about Murray, spoilin' your visit. You didn't mean any harm and...you should probably be off the island the first chance you get. Murray isn't the forgettin' kind."

She swung her long legs over the ledge of the window, the denim scratching faintly on the wood.

"Cleona isn't my great-grandmother," she said to the darkness.

"She isn't?" he asked incredulously. "Who is she?"

"She's my *great-great-great-great*-grandmother," she said softly. Then she brought her hand to her mouth, squishing the lips and skin between her fingers. She let out a ravaged sigh and moved out of sight.

"What?" he barked. "Wait!"

But she had already maneuvered herself soundlessly to the ground.

Ryan got up and peered out the window into the darkness, but could see nothing except the tumor of a moon. Even so, he stared out the window for the next few minutes, hoping to catch a glimpse of her.

He walked to his suitcase and picked up the rain jacket, turning it around and around in his hands. He emptied out the contents of his toiletry kit onto his bed. Then he ran his palm over the smooth cover of the textbook.

He calculated how old a person would have to be to be a grandmother to the fifth power. The number he came up with was impossibly comical.

He chuckled to himself. She must have been mistaken. Perhaps she was joking with him, having a laugh with Murray this very minute. Maybe she no longer knew truth from reality. He sighed, thinking what a pity it was when such beautiful women turned out to be a bit unhinged. *She could pose for more fashionable magazines than* Time, he thought.

He lay back on the bed, inhaling deeply of the lavender on the pillow. But he could only smell the turf smoke that Aisling left in her wake. His left leg began to cramp, and he jumped from the bed to stretch it out.

When he straightened up at last, he was surprised to hear movement in the previously empty room next door. He wondered if the room's occupant was just as disoriented as he was on this lost, little island.

6

Sister Ignatius sat in a faded armchair in her room at the hotel. The chair looked out a window at the island's southeastern end, which contained its one Catholic church, built in the late 19th century.

At least she had been given a room with a view.

The proprietor of the hotel, a middle-aged woman with four grown children and a dead husband, claimed to be Catholic. A poorly done painting of the Virgin Mary hung crookedly on one wallpapered wall, and a small metal cross bearing the Lord Jesus Christ hung over the door.

And yet, Sister Ignatius suspected that the island had a pagan heart beneath the veneer of Catholicism. She could see it in their wary eyes and hear it in their lyrical speech, the stubborn streak of lawlessness.

Her knee joints cracked as she rose from the chair; she held onto the padded arms as her head spun. Then she smoothed down her black habit, adjusted the coif and straightened her veil.

Her rosary beads rattled slightly on her way to the dining room, where the matron, Dorothy O'Sullivan, bustled about with dishes and pitchers.

"Morning, sister," she said loudly, filling a cup with black tea. "Did you sleep well?"

"No," she sighed. At that moment, Sister Ignatius wanted nothing more than to sit with her fellow sisters and eat the morning meal in silence.

"Oh," Dorothy said, wringing her hands in her apron. "Whatever was the matter?"

"It's my head," answered Sister Ignatius. "I have a cancer in my brain."

"Boys-a-dear!" breathed Dorothy, and crossed herself. "I'm so sorry for that. Sure, but after all of your service in God's name...it isn't right a-tall."

Sister Ignatius seated herself at a small table by the window. The water of the harbor glittered blindingly in the morning sun. "I wanted to spend some time by the sea. Before my symptoms get worse."

"Oh, aye, that's grand, sister," said Dorothy. Her face lit up. "It bein' such a lovely day and all, you should take a gander of the old church ruins, out by the cliffs. 'Tis nothing but a pile of rocks now, but the church was built atop a monastery, back in the 13th century. I've a pamphlet at the desk so, for the hikers. Our tour bus driver is on holiday, but I've got my husband's old car, the dodgy shambles that it is."

Sister Ignatius said nothing; she wasn't sure she wanted to see the island just yet. She hadn't left the cloistered monastery in almost fifty years, and just getting to the island had been a monumental effort for her.

Mother Superior had recommended the island for its austerity; she had heard that it fostered tranquility. But Sister Ignatius had been afraid, had prayed for strength to endure the trip alone.

And yet, she already felt different, here on the island. In spite of her weariness, she was reminded of an old feeling of hope, a buoyancy in her spirit that she'd felt when she was a young girl, pretending to be a priest.

She had presided over two stuffed sheep, which were really more like carcasses than animals. For the Sacraments, she had offered the creatures broken tea cups of water and torn pieces of used envelopes. She had then read passages from her mam's Bible. After the mass, she'd thought that the sheep looked healthier, more wholesome.

And she had carried that feeling with her when she was dodging her mam's drunken slaps. She had nurtured it during mass, inhaling her mam's hot, sweet breath. The priest's voice had carried over the congregation to the back of the church, where her family had always sat. The words had penetrated the haze of chaos and disappointment around them, making their way to her.

She had felt the power of her conviction growing inside her, a seed to a stem to a leaf. But her mam, an alcoholic mother amidst a village of pub-going fathers, had dismissed her desire, voiced confidently at supper at the age of ten, with a shout that Sister Ignatius had taken for a laugh.

"Women aren't allowed to be priests, you little eejit!" she'd yelled. Then, with glassy eyes and a wave of a floppy hand, her mam told her to clear the table, start on the dishes and put her baby sister in her crib.

Her mam had been right, for once.

But men, the gender deigned most appropriate to hold positions of power in the church, had abused their power with rampant sex abuse and generations of cowardly cover-ups. The Church had lost people's faith because men had been sneaking slaves to their own sexual needs.

And Sister Ignatius had never had such needs. She had barely even menstruated, and the change hadn't affected her at all, if only to widen her belly a bit. But billowing black was a blessed camouflage.

The women with whom she served amazed her every day; she now viewed men as weak creatures, unworthy of God's selection. But unfortunately, the pope felt differently. She prayed for him, but he was a man, after all.

Dorothy O'Sullivan placed a full plate of breakfast foods in front of her, interrupting the curdled trickles of thought. She looked up at the woman's red cheeks, her flyaway gray hair.

"I think I'd like to see the ruins today, if you have the time."

Dorothy smiled down at her and nodded, her eyes swimming with pity. "I'll fire up the car after breakfast."

Before Sister Ignatius ate, she prayed for several long minutes, even as the steam from the fried eggs and bangers teased her growling belly.

∞

Two hours later, Sister Ignatius gritted her teeth against the pain in her head as Dorothy maneuvered the old Peugeot along the pocked road toward the ruins.

"Stop. Stop the car," she gasped, her hand on the dashboard.

Dorothy screeched to a halt, and Sister Ignatius wrenched open the door and vomited her entire breakfast onto the gravel below.

"Am I driving too fast for you, sister?" cried Dorothy, pulling a handkerchief from her purse in the backseat.

"Yes," admitted Sister Ignatius, wiping her mouth and closing the car door.

Dorothy resumed driving so slowly that Sister Ignatius thought that even on foot she would have been able to keep up with the chugging car. Each pothole was navigated with careful maneuvering; there were seemingly dozens of them.

She soon noticed the green, rocky hills dotted with small lakes, the homes, connected with electric lines, scattered about the brown fields. Soon, she saw the ocean in front of them. For the eight decades that she'd lived in Ireland, itself an island, she'd never once seen the Atlantic.

Dorothy parked the car at a mound of rocks near the cliffs at the edge of the island and hurried around to help Sister Ignatius out. The light breeze flipped the ends of Sister Ignatius's veil as she gazed about. The church had completely disintegrated, its original purpose unrecognizable.

She felt a sob bubble in her throat. Perhaps she shouldn't have come to the ruins after all, she thought.

The mess was a sad symbol of the golden age in which Ireland, following the death of St. Patrick in 493 AD, became the most important religious center in Europe. Some Irish monks had roamed about Europe on their first missions, converting the pagan tribes of Britain and establishing monasteries in France and Italy. Other monks wanted more solitude, and found refuge on the western islands of Europe.

"I'd like to stay here by myself awhile," said Sister Ignatius.

"Go away on with you! That's a terrible notion," declared Dorothy, hands planted on her big hips. "What if you throw off again and there's no one to help you? I don't want it said that I left a sick nun by the ruins, just like a moldy sack of potatoes. You know how the people do talk, sister."

"If you could fetch me in an hour, would that suit you?" she asked. "I'd like to take some photos." She pulled from a habit pocket the case with the camera that Mother Superior had given her for her trip. She hoped she would remember how to use it.

Dorothy puzzled over that for a few moments. "Now, don't go exertin' yourself, sister. Just sit down on this rock and take your photos. I can help with gettin' 'em developed, so. I'll be back in one hour on the mark."

"Thank you."

Sister Ignatius smiled, watching the Peugeot bump back down the road at a breakneck pace. The gulls, disturbed at the whine of the engine, looped tight ovals above. Her belly empty, she felt her soul more clearly—a better, holier version of herself that she knew from praying with the sisters in the monastery's chapel before the sun was even up. The peace induced within her a soporific release, and she closed her eyes, grateful for the sun's warmth.

Yet almost immediately, her back began to ache from sitting on the slab of rock, so she got up and gripping the camera case, walked carefully among the stones. The monks that lived here so long ago must have created lives of ordered contemplation, she thought. They must have heard God's word clearly, for He was near. She swallowed thickly, her mouth still tasting of vomited eggs.

She stepped through weeds and briars, snagging her habit, as she made her way to the cliffs. Signs in both Gaelic and English warned tourists to watch their step, for the cliffs descended perilously to the pounding ocean below.

She peeked over the jagged edge to see the foamy surf arching into the air. She drew in a breath and watched the ocean make its inevitable way toward the cliffs. She said a quick prayer, for the way that the ocean carved the rock so diligently, so forcefully, made her long for the blind love of God. Looking down at the frothing sea, at the ravaged cliff sides, she could almost see God's face.

She wanted to feel that same oceanic energy again, the way she felt when she was a child. The feeling had been lost, through the decades of routine and service and loneliness. Her pride, her ambition, had gradually been worn down.

She thought perhaps the cancer had been born from that long lost pride. For months her head had pained her so badly, sometimes every day, so that finally Mother Superior had taken her to see a neurologist. The doctor had told her that the malignant tumor, found in the most delicate part of the frontal lobe of her brain, was inoperable.

He'd briefed her and Mother Superior on the other symptoms she could expect to experience in the coming weeks and months: nausea and vomiting, behavioral and emotional changes, impaired judgment, memory loss, paralysis on one side of the body, reduced mental capacity, and vision loss, not to mention the increased possibility of stroke.

She and Mother Superior had taken the news stoically; they had known each other for over sixty years, when Mother Superior had been Sister Gabriel, the embodiment of proper sisterly conduct. She had told Sister Ignatius, "The Lord has a plan for you." She had sent Sister Ignatius to the island with money the sisters had raised by selling a staggering amount of baked goods to the diocese.

Now that she was here, the island spoke to her, the same way that God did—quietly, reverently. She listened, and heard the rush of the ocean, the hushing of a protective mother. She smelled the sea on her habit's sleeves, on the skin of her hands, and she knew that it was God himself.

She prayed there, on the edge of the cliff, for strength, for guidance in these last months of life. Then she removed the camera from its case, turned it on, aimed it down, and pushed the button, hoping that her finger hadn't obscured the view.

7

———————

Despite the warmth of the night, Aisling shivered, slightly hysterical. She knew the road, even in darkness, but tonight her legs led her to Kiley's father's dilapidated barn.

The barn was empty now, for Kiley's father was no longer a farmer or even a fisherman. He, like most everyone else on the island, was a pensioner, and spent most of his nights in the pub.

Aisling collapsed on the earth of old Jimmy's stall. Jimmy had been a sweet, even-tempered donkey, but he had long since died, the last of the family's animals to be worn out by work. The stall still smelled of his manure and sweat, a reminder of childhood, of time in the barn with Kiley.

With no parents to raise her, and two old women as her guardians, Aisling ran wild as a youngster. By the time she was five years old, she'd figured the island out—until she'd encountered Kiley. They had met on a vacant stretch of beach, exactly halfway in the middle of the island. Each girl had brought along a little rake and a bucket for collecting cockles.

Aisling recalled Kiley's smudged face, untidy blonde hair and toothpick legs, unlikely matched with a superior attitude. No sooner had she spotted Aisling than she'd toed a line through the sand and said, "Watch where you step. This part of the beach is mine."

Ailsing had marched right up to the line and messed it up with her bare feet.

Kiley, apparently surprised by the bravado, stuck out her chest and said, "My da told me about you. You're that girleen who lives with the witches."

"They are *not* witches."

It had been the first she'd heard of the islander's opinions of them. It wouldn't be the last.

"Don't be thinkin' of castin' any spells on me. I can chuck a stone clear across this beach and hit that big rock over there."

Aisling had laughed. "Let's see it then."

Kiley had searched around her feet for a good stone. Then she had reared back her skinny arm and let the stone fly. It had flown expertly through the air and hit the rock with a loud crack, and Aisling had looked on the girl with admiration.

"Now who's castin' spells," she'd said.

"You shouldn't mess about with me, is all I'm sayin'."

The two girls had worked side by side all day, Aisling spinning tale after tale as their rakes clanged dully against the cockle shells in the sand. When the sun slipped into the sea, they vowed to meet again the next day. Kiley had promised to teach Aisling how to throw a stone properly, and Aisling had promised to tell more stories.

Aisling, with her natural strength and good vision, had learned to throw a stone even better than Kiley, much to Kiley's consternation. Aisling never seemed to get sick, either, even when the entire island was sniffling and sneezing to death.

And yet, when all of the island girls had started their menses, Aisling had remained as flat-chested and bloodless as a young boy. By the time she was 18 years old, Aisling had still not started her bleeding. The humiliating detail had leaked out when Kiley had bemoaned the lack of sanitary pads on the island. Aisling had asked what a pad was.

"You haven't got your period a-tall?" Kiley had screeched, causing the cow to knock about in her stall. "You're eighteen years old!"

"Cleona says it isn't important," Aisling had shrugged. "She told me that she came into her womanhood late too. Same with my mam."

"Jesus, Mary and Joseph," Kiley had marveled. She studied Aisling's body for a full minute. "It's the fairy blood in you."

Aisling had rolled her eyes. "I'm perfectly happy not to bleed like a stuck pig from between my legs every month."

"Well, at least I can have babies," Kiley had said, spiking up her short, blonde hair with both hands.

"You want a clutch of babies, do you?"

"Not yet," she'd admitted. "But I'm thinking of becoming a nanny soon. I'm good with children, so I am."

"There are only seven children on the island, and they're all scared of you."

"So? Doesn't mean I'm not good with the cursed snappers."

Aisling held her breath. "But who would pay you to be a nanny on *this* island?"

"I'd be nanny in *Dublin*. People pay top dollar for nannies in Dublin. I've looked into it."

"But then...you'd live in Dublin."

"Aye."

Ailsing's body itched. "Are you going to go, Kiley?"

"I have to. I'm bored to death on this island. If you'd have come with me to school, you'd know what a pit this island really is."

After grammar school, Kiley had left the island to attend boarding school, 60 miles away, on the mainland. Aisling had chosen to forgo the extra education and take care of Cleona and Catherine. She had missed Kiley, of course, but she'd still come back to the island for long holidays. Aisling had learned to be patient for companionship.

"You could come with me, you know," Kiley had said. "It would do you good."

"I could never leave the island," Aisling had said, shaking her head. "It's home."

"Some home!" Kiley had snorted. "A bunch of old farts drinking away the dole in the pub every night!"

"But won't you miss it just a little bit?" Aisling had tried before to imagine a world of endless land, a place with no view of the ocean, and she had seen only a lifeless stretch of dry grey. She had seen nothing, no one. And she had heard no stories in her head.

Kiley snorted. "I'll be back for holidays still."

She then began scraping at the remains of purple polish on her finger nails. "I worry about you, you know, being so peculiar. A woman with your good looks would do well on the mainland. Better than a poor fisherman like Murray."

"I'm not marryin' Murray."

There were four families with young children on the island.

But it had been many long years since a couple had married on the island itself, and Murray didn't seem in a hurry to break with the trend.

"Who *are* you going to marry, then? Padraig O'Riley?"

Aisling had laughed in spite of herself. Padraig O'Riley was a red-haired, middle-aged drunk that lived in a falling-down cottage in the West Village. He wandered the island, muttering darkly to himself, and when he chanced to bump into Aisling on the road, he screamed like a little girl and ran away as fast as a track star.

In Kiley's infrequent postcards, she wrote in English of music, of new friends, of motorcycle-riding boyfriends, of fashion. They told of sushi and hybrid cars and wine bars, of many things that kept her from coming home. Aisling had saved them all, and still read them by the lamp almost every night, even though they were in the unfamiliar language.

On a visit last summer, dressed in a black leather jacket, Kiley had even brought Aisling a pair of tight, denim trousers exactly like the ones that Kiley herself had been wearing. Aisling now wore them every day, much to the dismay of Cleona. They were getting a bit worn in the knees and rear, but she planned to patch them when they finally ripped open.

Aisling had thought to write to Kiley a few months ago, when she had finally gotten her period, at the age of twenty-five. But she'd decided it wasn't the sort of thing one wrote in a letter.

∞

She left the barn and made her way back home, the full moon lighting the road enough to see Murray, standing at the gate to her cottage in the exact spot where Ryan Abernathy had stood not eight hours ago.

"Where you been, girl?" he called. He still wore his oilskin trousers, tucked into rubber boots.

"Out walkin', if it's any business of yours."

Murray did many things for Aisling. Without Murray, Aisling didn't know how she, or the old women, would get by. When the fishing slowed, and he wasn't parked on a stool in the pub, he helped her in her small field, planting and sowing her crop of potatoes, carrots, onions and lettuce. He fetched mussel shells and seaweed, to supplement her small supply of manure, and spread it over the field. He cut turf for them, brought her driftwood to add to the fire. He brought them fish and crab and lobster from his hauls, wool shorn from his sheep.

She had allowed him to kiss her on a handful of occasions, but his weathered lips swiped like sandpaper, his tongue lay like a dead slug in her mouth. He kissed without passion, so that she wondered on the working order of his willy.

"Out walkin'? Seems like you're always out walkin'. Do you ever get any place is the question."

"It's not the gettin' of places I'm concerned over."

He closed the distance between them in two easy strides. He grabbed her hand and said, "What *are* you concerned over?"

His eyes darted over her face, then behind her and all about the cottage.

She slipped her hand from his grip. "Cleona, of course. And Catherine."

Murray straightened his back and nodded. "Sure you are. I know that. How is the old girl today, after the Yank came a-callin'?"

"She's not well," she mumbled.

"What was he wantin' about her age, anyways?"

"He's a scientist," she said. "He wants to study her, I guess."

"She shouldn't be conversin' with outsiders," he scolded. "Nosy saps like him especially."

"She welcomed his company," she said. "She's starved for visitors."

"Some visitor! Did you see the looks of that pack he was carryin'?" Murray jeered. "What do you reckon was inside that thing?"

"Books," she said.

He snorted. "Well, a lot of good they did him," he said, grabbing her elbow and steering her down the road. "I've got something to show you."

"I'm not at myself, Murray," said Aisling, dragging her booted feet in the gravel.

"Och, I'll have none of your mopin'."

"And why aren't you at the pub, anyways?" she asked.

"Already been," he said. When he laughed, she smelled stale beer on his breath.

Murray led her to his own cottage down the road from Aisling's, where he lived with his mother, Mary Finnegan. The family had lived in the West Village for many generations, and Murray and his older sister Moira, who still lived in the cottage, were the last Finnegans on the island. His older brother Liam had left a decade ago to work on an off-shore commercial fishing ship. Aisling had forgotten what he looked like, but he still sent money to his mother every month.

Mary, a glaring, wild-haired woman, did nothing but gaze out the window all day. Aisling saw her round, white face peering out whenever she walked by. When she was younger, Aisling used to wave to her, but Mary had never once waved back, so Aisling now kept her arms at her sides when walking by the cottage. Mary refused to allow Aisling into the house, so Aisling had never seen the inside of it. She'd seen plenty of the barn, though.

He opened the barn door and led her inside, where Aisling heard Murray's dozen or so sheep milling about. He lit the lamp that hung on the inside wall of the barn and shone it on a dark lump on the dirt below. After a few seconds, Aisling could see that it was two dead gray seals. She smelled the blood and the sea water on their skins, drawing flies in the heat of the barn.

"Murray, what have you done?" she breathed.

He stuck out his chest. "They got tangled up in our trawlin' net today," he said. "We had to shoot 'em."

"You shouldn't have done it," she said.

"They'll eat up all the fish, woman. They're terrible hard on our livelihoods, so if you're goin' to feel sorry for somethin', it should be me comin' home with no fish in the nets."

She closed her eyes and tried not to breathe. "What are you plannin' on doin' with 'em?"

He shrugged. "I thought I might try eatin' 'em. Me granddad once told me seal meat is the best kind of meat there is, full of oil and chock full of the flavor. As good as pork."

Aisling's stomach turned, and she backed out of the barn. She murmured, "No one eats seal meat anymore. And it's illegal altogether."

"I'll be happy to bring some over. I'll bet Cleona would like a taste of it."

She thought he was probably right. Seal meat was once a sought-after meal on the Celtic islands, and oil had been extracted from the seal's liver to use in healing wounds. It had long gone out of favor as a food though.

More than anything though, Cleona respected their mystery, their place in myth. Aisling always felt fortunate to catch one slipping through the water. When she came across a seal, especially at night, she believed the myths that described the "selkies"—part seal, part human—as shape-shifters, only able to make human contact with one person for a short amount of time before they had to return to the sea as a seal.

Looking into a seal's soulful eyes, Aisling believed in her history, in the power of her blood. She knew that anything was possible on the island, and she felt satisfied for a while.

∞

Murray walked Aisling back to her cottage through the ghostly village. Wide awake but sapped of strength, Aisling sat on the front stoop and wound her long hair between her hands. Murray sat down beside her and draped a heavy arm over her shoulders.

"I want to talk to you," he said quietly.

Aisling's body stiffened. Murray was one of the few young men left on the island, and even he was gone a lot of the time, fishing off the island coasts with a crew of locals twice his age. And like the ones who ended up eventually leaving, Murray was frustrated by his life's dearth of promise. He lacked education, and fishing was his only skill, so he spent his nights in the pub, moaning along with the island's elderly cast-offs. Worst of all, he was a talented fiddler and singer, but he rarely performed on the island any more.

"If Cleona dies..." he began.

"Murray Finnegan! Don't even say it!"

He put a hand on her head, drawing her closer to him. She smelled the fish and blood on his oilskin trousers. "Now listen, girl. I'm trying to plan things out, now."

She shook her head. "No. Not now."

"Now is the time," he urged. "She's dyin', Aisling."

"No. She's just sick is all."

"She's old." He paused for a few moments, shifted his rubber boots on the dirt. "And what will become of the cottage when she passes on?"

She didn't speak; she couldn't imagine the house empty of Cleona, the heft of her years.

"It will go to you. As will the land."

"It's just a little scrap of land."

"It's plenty. It could be a good start for us, is what I'm sayin'."

She sighed. "And what will become of your mam?"

"Well, I'm not goin' to abandon the woman, am I? I'll see to her. And anyways, she still has Moira."

He stroked her cheek with a rough hand. "I want to live with *you*, girl."

"Why?"

"Keep you away from the scientists!"

"Why, Murray?" she asked softly.

"Oh, you know," he said, struggling for words. "Known you my whole life and all. It's only right we should live together. As man and wife."

She bit her lip. He had finally, in a round-about fashion, mentioned marriage. She tried to imagine a life spent with a man who killed seals, a man who disliked stories that didn't include war and blood, a man who enjoyed his drinking mates more than a good kiss.

She stood up. "I'm goin' to bed."

He sighed mightily, and tried to pull her back down by tugging on her hand. "You forgot somethin', girl."

She glared down at him until he stood up.

He pulled her to him roughly, then mashed his sun-dried lips into hers. He stuck his hands in the back pockets of her jeans and squeezed her buttocks, a rare overture. As his tongue pushed thickly into her mouth, she thought of Murray as a child, the way she always did when he kissed her.

Like most of the island children, he'd been scared of her. He would hide in the fields or the barn whenever she walked by his cottage. When he grew a bit older, he would throw rocks at her from his hiding places, would yell out ugly, hateful things. It was only when she'd grown into a woman that he'd shown any interest in her. She'd always pretended not to remember his former behavior, and now, wrapped in a tight, meaty embrace, she regretted it.

She pulled away from him roughly and opened the door of her cottage.

"Go on, now. It's late."

She closed the door, more forcefully than she really needed to.

∞

For the few hours remaining in the night, Aisling didn't sleep at all, perched up in the warm loft above Cleona's bed. Her down-filled mattress offered no comfort. She listened to the loud gurgling from the chest of Cleona with a feeling of doom.

Before the sun had even risen, Aisling had swept yesterday's ashes from the hearth, added the last of the driftwood to the fire, filled the oil lamps, and emptied the toilet and slop buckets. Carrying a basket, she walked next door to see to Catherine, who was still asleep, snoring softly, her gummy mouth wide open. She added some wood to the fire, filled a cup with water, and placed it and a plate of bread on a rough table beside her bed. Then she went out to their little barn to milk the cow and fetch some eggs from the henhouse for breakfast.

Cleona had told Aisling that her family used to keep a cow and pig in the kitchen, to keep the beasts warm. She'd said that when she was a girl, she would climb onto the roof and dig through the thatches for freshly laid eggs, for the hens found the reeds a good place to lay.

But now the hens were tucked into a little house, and Aisling was sorry that they couldn't explore the way that their ancestors did. She was glad, however, that the cow spent her days and nights in the barn.

On her way back to the cottage, Aisling paused, the eggs in her apron. It was still very early in the morning, and there wasn't a noise to be heard, other than the ocean's swill. It was usually Aisling's favorite time of day, when the darkness was standing on the threshold, kissing the earth goodbye. Once the sun arrived, the magic of the day disintegrated.

She well knew that the day was October 31. In the old Celtic days, it was known as Samhain, a harvest festival marking the death of an old year and the beginning of a new one. The earth would move from a season of light to a season of darkness, and the people would turn inward, preparing for light and life to return. The day itself was a time of unrest; spirits, fairy folk and goblins were said to enter the break in the veil separating the worlds of the dead and the living, and they would visit their living relatives with either good or bad intentions.

Aisling had loved the day since she was a small girl, for the stories that she cherished would come alive. She would look over her shoulder all day for the spirits of her mother and father, for the other ancestors she had heard so much about.

But the warm spell had spoiled her expectations, dulling her body and mind both. She could only see the dead seals in Murray's barn. She could still smell their stench in her hair. Perhaps she would wash it in the stream, a summer habit forgotten until today.

On her way inside, she almost dropped the eggs from her apron when she found Cleona seated at the hearth, dressed in her special red petticoat and wool jacket. Her pale face shone with happiness, or perhaps it was perspiration from the effort of dressing herself.

"You're up so early, *Mamo*," she said, taking the eggs out and placing them carefully on the table.

She hurried over to her chair. "You should have waited for me to help you."

"It's my favorite time of year," she whispered. She coughed into a handkerchief as Aisling hovered.

Cleona finally settled and looked to Aisling. "What is it, my girl? Thinking of the handsome Yank?"

"It's nothing," she tried to smile. The palm she laid on Cleona's forehead burned. "I'm just tired."

"Nothing a little hard work won't cure."

"I still have to fetch the water," Aisling said, lingering beside Cleona.

"Good girl. Clear your head."

Aisling kissed her on her fevered cheek, quickly grabbed the water buckets and placed a towel and a cake of soap in one of them. She left Cleona to gaze out the front window on the fields and the sea, still hidden in darkness.

A long time ago, Cleona and her husband Brian lived in this very home with their one surviving child, a daughter called Eavan. Cleona had told Aisling about the hardships of their early life—the disputes with landlords, the crushing poverty and struggle for any kind of food: gull's eggs, found in the crevices of the cliffs, rabbits caught with a snare, lobster roe eaten from fists while fishing, seaweed and limpets and periwinkles, eaten raw.

She told Aisling that she used to help pull Brian's curragh through the merciless waves onto the strand, would help haul the nets in too, full of fish. The sea water would completely soak her wool dress, and she would hang it near the fire to dry, her entire body aching from the effort of it all. But she said that she would rather help him like that than watch, from her perch on the cliffs, the three men methodically rowing out to sea, for they always appeared so small to her, nothing more than toys in the sea's monstrous hands.

Cleona had had to travel to the mainland for flour, but she'd baked her own bread. She fetched turf on the hills with her donkey, tended their many sheep, and spun her own wool for knitting; she farmed their land full of vegetables, with Eavan toddling beside her with her own basket. When Eavan had a daughter of her own—Fiona—the three generations of women worked in the fields and the house, dawn to dusk, day after day.

She told tales of dancing sets on summer evenings in the homes of both West and East Villagers, where she often charmed visitors with stories. Cleona enjoyed visitors very much, especially when they paid calls to her cottage to hear her stories. The visitors were called *la breaghs*, which in English means "fine day."

In Aisling's cottage, there had been singing and music and a sense of unity, and Aisling marveled how much the heart of the island had really changed, had become through the decades a place primarily for foreigners, while the local people that still lived here became invisible, subservient, more and more reliant on family members in America, as well as government assistance. Now, there was dancing and music in the community center about once a month, heavy drinking in the pub.

Aisling wondered what Cleona recalled from those long-ago days when she gazed out the window. She had been happy, among her sorrows, she had told Aisling as much. But after so much life, her mind, and now her body, were slowly giving out, and Aisling hated to leave her alone now. She picked up speed as she ran down the hills toward the stream, her buckets swinging wildly at her sides.

When she arrived at the stream, she removed her sweater, and kneeling by the water's edge, she dipped her long hair into the gurgling coolness. Still bent, she rubbed the rosemary soap between her hands and worked the lather into her dripping locks. Then she rinsed it all out by pouring a bucket of water onto her head. She rubbed her hair with the towel and then stood up, grabbing for her sweater.

As she pulled her wet head through the neck, she saw a man, walking through the meadow toward her. There was just enough light for her to see that it was Ryan Abernathy, with his crop of heroic hair, and she had the urge to hide from him, to run away. But her fingers still remembered what that hair had felt like yesterday. She could smell his lavender smell, even over the haze of rosemary all about her. It reminded her of spring, and hope.

"What are you doing here?"

"Looking for you." He took a couple of steps toward her.

She rubbed her hair roughly with the damp towel again. "Why? I told you enough last night."

"No," he shook his head. She could see his eyes behind the glasses, watching her carefully. "Not nearly enough."

"I thought you would have been gone by now."

He looked down. "I'm sorry I ambushed you like this. I just... haven't been able to get your words out my mind. I hardly slept. I mean, I'm not an expert at genealogy, but that many number of greats..."

She placed a bucket in the water and scooped the cold water into it. He tried to help her with the second bucket, but she pulled it from his hands.

"How?" he asked. "How can it be true? It can't be."

She looked about her at the vacant hills, then back at his brown eyes, fringed by thick eyelashes. "Carry this," she said, giving him one of the water buckets. She stuffed the soap into the towel and carried the bundle in her other hand.

She led him down the grassy meadow to find the low road that ran along the beaches. They crunched along the vacant pathway in silence, and her head grew cool as the stream water left her hair. Soon, she spotted the scattered stones on the hillside.

She left the road and climbed across the damp, weedy grass to the remains of the church. She sat down on a low wall of stones, close to the cliffs. Ryan made his way over to her, occasionally exclaiming over the briars that snatched at his nice pants.

Aisling tried to breathe deeply as she gazed out to sea. Normally, being alone on the cliffs affirmed her view of the world as a small place, simple and good. If only the wind was blowing, or the mist was slowly seeping into her hair, she might have felt better. She searched her mind for the proper English, gathered the words together.

He finally sat down beside her, as quietly watchful as the gulls nearby. He was waiting for her to give him the answers he seemed to want very badly.

"The monastery was built over a thousand years ago. Then the church was built on top of its ruins," she said, still looking at the sea. "And now, it's ruins again, sure enough. One day the ocean will take it all, mark my words. There used to be a few hundred meters of land in front of us, but it's all shorn away now."

She saw him sideways, as he ran a hand over a pocked stone beside him. The gulls cried from the crevices in the cliffs below. The sun's rays had found their backs, there on the edge of the island. The growing heat muddled her mind.

She squeezed her eyes shut. "Cleona, Catherine and me...we have old blood."

She abruptly got up. She knew that she was going to tell him the story, the story that she knew best of all. But she would have to go slowly.

She stepped to another crumbled wall and sat down. She rested her face between her knees, feeling the soft denim rub her cheeks. Ryan followed, and sat down next to her.

"Tell me more," he urged. "What does that mean?"

She could hardly hear her own voice. "The lines of our family stretch back thousands of years. We are descended from an old island clan."

"A clan," he repeated. "How do you know that?"

"How?" She shrugged. "The stories."

Ryan sniffed, looked down at his hands.

"Cleona says that at one time, there were over 300 of us here with the same blood. Now it's only us, so it is." She paused to run a line with a finger in the dry dirt. "There may be more, but we're scattered to the winds now."

"Where did they go?" His tone was doubtful, even playful.

"Everywhere. Some left the island for food and money and easier lives. But many died, you know. It's a hard life, here. And some had trouble..."

She couldn't continue.

"So what are you saying?" he asked. "Does extreme age run in your family or something? I don't understand."

She got up and walked over to the buckets, grabbing handles in both hands. She couldn't tell him the story after all—it wasn't coming out right.

"I have to go. Cleona is awake," she said.

He nodded his head in defeat, stood up easily on his long legs. "How is she today?" he asked.

"She's in good spirits," she answered, her throat tightening over the truth bubbling forth. "But she's very sick."

She turned, but he held a hand out to her. "Wait, Aisling! Please...Can I see Cleona again? Will you help me? I just need one DNA sample from her. And one from Catherine. Then I'll be on my way."

His glasses caught the light of the rising sun, and the sight of him, so hopeful amidst the ruins, made her smile. He seemed familiar to her, somehow, a visitor from the split in the veil.

"Aye. Come back at noon today. You can take a meal with us."

She made her way down the hill, feeling the way that she did when she spotted a seal, sunbathing on a rock—that everything around her was filled with magic, that the world was a special place.

8

———

Ryan watched Aisling walk back to the village, the buckets of water sloshing her jeans with each stride. As masses of black-backed gulls circled overhead, he gazed after her until she resembled a stick of willow at the bottom of the meadow, and then she disappeared into the hills.

Eyes still lingering, he thought of Amanda Langley, a college hook-up of his. Aisling and Amanda shared the same long limbs, but that was where their similarities ended. Amanda had designer clothing and a red BMW that reeked of her expensive perfume, and she would have killed herself with her manicure scissors before carrying buckets of washing water back to an earthen-floor cottage that she shared with her great-grandmother.

But a hormonally infested Ryan had lusted after the back of Amanda's glossy blonde head when she had sat in front of him in a mandatory Spanish 101 class. After rare persistence on Ryan's part, she had finally taken his virginity in the heated back seat of her car. They hadn't even kissed, and Ryan had reeked of her perfume for days afterward.

Following the encounter, he'd entrenched himself in his studies, and the back of Amanda's head had never again appealed to him. He'd marveled how it ever had.

Now, he could feel similar longings, awakening from a petrified sleep. Aisling's red eyelashes had glittered in the strong morning light, and droplets of water had slowly meandered down the hills of her breasts, hidden beneath that sweater, and he had suddenly wanted to touch her lightly freckled face.

But, he told himself, he shouldn't do anything that would jeopardize his chances of getting the samples. And the things that she'd told him didn't make any sense; he had a strong feeling that she had made it all up, perhaps in an effort to tease him, or deceive him.

He heard Rose and Dr. Buxton in his head, telling him to come home, to face the fact that some centenarians were just too sick, or too forgetful, to work with, that the island was another lost cause.

But he didn't want to return to America yet.

∞

When Aisling was long out of sight, Ryan began to walk down the high road toward the East Village. As his feet ground the broken asphalt, he imagined walking in the footsteps of the Celtic islanders of old—the clan, as she'd described it.

He didn't know much about clans. From recent genetic studies on the people of the British Isles, he'd learned that a clan was a group of related people, claiming a common ancestor. But the term "clan" sounded far removed from everyday reality. A clan was the stuff of old, forgotten stories, told to the sound of bagpipes and flutes.

Ryan stopped walking and pulled out the brochure that he'd taken from the front desk and sat down on a wall of stones. He'd scanned the brochure this morning, to find the most likely stream that Aisling used to get her water, and had seen something about the early history of the island.

He read it again, more thoroughly. Somewhere to his left lay an area that was rich in prehistoric remains, mainly the 4,000-year-old foundations of stone terracing, cooking pits and house sites. Together with the nearby field systems, they suggested intensive farming and a large population. The island had been inhabited for a very long time.

Ryan looked up from the brochure. The fields now looked half-cultivated, a picture of subsistence farming. The call of the outside world had pulled the inhabitants away from the hard life of agriculture and fishing; electric lines looped across the land. But he could see the ocean from every direction. At least *that* fact hadn't changed in four millennia.

Ryan shaded his eyes to watch the gulls overhead.

If there had been a clan on the island, he imagined that they would have had different ideas and values than the people of mainland Europe. They must have even looked differently, acted differently, ate differently. He also wondered if, in their isolation, they *made* themselves different, a kind of "longevity eugenics" scheme that resulted in a bunch of long-lived people, whose descendants still lived on the island.

He laughed to himself at the idea. It made for a good story.

∞

On the way to the hotel, Ryan passed by the pub near the harbor, and since the door was propped open with a rock, he thought to look inside. A gray-haired man already worked a mop along the floor behind the pocked wood of the bar. He stopped to take a sip from a steaming mug by the cash register, when he noticed Ryan standing in the doorway.

"We're closed," he called cheerfully.

"My apologies," said Ryan, and turned to leave.

But to Ryan's surprise, the man called, "Oh, it's yourself, is it? Come in, come in!"

"Uh...I don't want to impose."

"Bullocks!" the man said, swatting the air. "You're the Yank Dorothy told me about. You're very welcome."

Ryan walked tentatively into the dark bar and sat down on a cracked leather stool. Smiling broadly, the man filled a glass with dark beer and set in on the bar in front of Ryan. He leaned on his mop as he gazed at him. He had thinning hair, and a stained shirt with buttons straining over his paunch.

"Tell me, is it lost treasure you're huntin'?" he asked.

"No, nothing like that," said Ryan, but then wondered on the truth of it.

"Every so often, the island gets bits and pieces of the past, washed up on its shores and beggin' for stories to be told of it. Viking helmets, jewels of the finest stones, spears and shields and all manner of English soldiering goods: buttons, rifles, things like that. The hikers scour the sand for hours on a day."

"A few years ago, that would have interested me."

"So, is it business you're after?" the man asked,

unwilling to let the matter go. "Land speculatin'? I won't sell, but I know of a few men that might, given the right price."

"Well, at *first* it was business...it's all a mess now." He took a deep pull of the beer.

"Sure, sounds like you met up with the Good People!" he said jovially.

"Who are they?"

The man snickered and shook his head. "The fairy folk! They don't cause us too much trouble, but they get a bit frisky on Halloween, so."

"Well, I'll take that into consideration," smiled Ryan. "I *did* meet an intriguing woman in the West Village, though."

The man twiddled the handle of the mug with his white-haired fingers. "Did you, now?"

Ryan's tongue formed words on its own. "Perhaps you know Cleona Owen?"

The man hesitated a few moments before answering. "Course I know her. Lived here my whole life. I know the entire island *and* their livestock."

He busied himself with unpacking boxes of bottles, no further information given. Ryan slipped some euros onto the bar, more than he felt comfortable offering.

"I'd like to know more about her."

The man eyed the money, then grunted. He continued unpacking, but after a couple of minutes, he put a wrinkled hand over the money and put it in the pocket of a grimy apron hanging on a peg.

He stacked the boxes inside each other and retreated through a back door for a few minutes. When he returned, he said, almost to himself, "She's powerful sick, I do know that. Won't live out the month, so I heard."

Then, in a low voice, he said, "Me granddad knew Cleona. Always had a kind word to say of her."

He sipped from his mug, his eyes unfocused with thought. "She's of the old ways."

A stooped, skinny man peeked his bald head through the back door and trilled, "Hey now, Donal, I'm trick or treatin', so I am. Could you spare a wee treat this grand mornin'?"

"Away off and chase yourself," he yelled. "Can't you see I'm conductin' business here?"

"Oh, mighty sorry. Right you are. I'll trot along and come back later."

The man called Donal shook his head sadly at Ryan. "The drouth can't get by without a morning pint, holiday or not."

He grabbed his mop, but his eyes stared at a point beyond Ryan's head. "Owen is an old island family, so they are. Been here for ages."

Donal bowed his head, as if he were praying. "And Cleona was old, even to my grandfather."

"That doesn't make any sense," Ryan said, not willing to play the part of the naïve tourist.

The man shrugged and began to mop half-heartedly.

"She can't be that old!"

"Nothing that strange about bein' old," he said. "This island has always been full of the old. We don't think much about it."

"How old is old here?" His voice was louder than he meant it to be. His mind fished around for proven facts. "The oldest living person is 114 years old, and she lives in Okinawa, Japan." Ryan had met her, when they'd visited Okinawa, but he now had a hard time recalling her face.

Donal nodded. "She's powerful old."

"Yes, but from what you said about your grandfather, it sounds as if Cleona is even older than that!"

Ryan thought he saw a little smile on his chapped lips as he ducked his head below the bar and rattled some bottles around.

He said to the balding top of the man's head, "I'm sorry, I'm just...trying to understand. To find out the truth."

"The truth," the man repeated, emerging with a full bottle of whiskey.

He poured a good measure of the brown liquid into his mug. Ryan produced some more euros, and the man grinned as he put the bills into the apron pocket.

He took a sip of the concoction and leaned in close, his eyes sparkling. "We say there's magic afoot out there."

Ryan shook his head. "I don't believe in magic. I'm a scientist."

"There's nothing else for it," the man said firmly, drinking the rest of the mug's contents. "But Cleona's cheerful, not a thing she wouldn't do for you, if she could, so she gets along here. But Catherine—that's her sister, now—she's a different story altogether. Some think she's a witch, and to tell you the truth, I'm not a-tall sure she's not. One day she wasn't here, and then one day she was, and the spitting image of Cleona. It's magic, I tell you."

"You know they're twins," said Ryan. "Twin sisters."

He felt the way that he did when he was speaking with a centenarian with advanced dementia.

"Aye, that's what they say," Donal said, obviously not

convinced.

Donal's face slackened, and he went on. "Once upon a time, it wasn't so unusual to be related to your neighbor, on an island such as this. Those women come from a long line of close relations, and some say it's made them strange."

Ryan pondered the more scientific explanation a while, finishing his beer. He took out some more euros. "And what about Aisling? Is she a witch too?"

Donal cackled at him. "Ah, it's Aisling you're asking of now. I should have known it."

Donal took the money and put it in the pocket. "Aisling, as you can see, is a lovely girl. And a good girl to take care of her elderly relations like she does. But she's always been a bit queer. Slow. Simple, you know. If it hadn't been for Kiley MacSheehan watchin' out for her all those years, I don't want to guess how she'd have fared out here."

"Kiley is a friend of hers?"

"Aye, and a wilder girleen I've never seen on this island. She lives in Dublin now, and I do miss the sight of that spiked-up hair and red lips. Aisling near took the rickets when she left. The women here don't take to her, you know."

The man slowly ran a rag over the same spot of the bar. Finally, he said, "Aisling's mother, Orla, went to the grammar school with me. Aisling's the spitting image of her—gifted with the beauty. All the men wanted her, but she only had eyes for her cousin Michael."

"Her *cousin*?" asked Ryan.

He nodded. "Aye. 'Twas her third or fourth cousin once removed. But they never married."

"Why not?"

Donal shrugged. "It's just the way, out here."

Ryan took a big sip of beer.

Donal continued. "Orla had a devil of a time with the babies. Then she died giving birth to Aisling, in the same cottage where they now live. Lots of their women came to the same end, as it is. Then Aisling's father Michael—who had become a great strong fisherman—died in the storm not too long after. No one could believe the luck."

"And Aisling?"

"Cleona raised her up. Well, really, 'twas Aisling that raised her own self. Cleona and Catherine were old, you know. Poor as church mice, could barely put food in their bellies, but were too proud to go on the scratch."

Ryan nodded, but his mind couldn't grasp the facts of the conversation. Perhaps the beer was muddling him. And Donal's voice was melodic, the words almost indistinguishable, an endless stream.

"People say that a lovestruck local boy named Tommy Coyne tried to follow her to her cottage one rainy spring afternoon, but she disappeared into the mist right in front of his eyes. He heard the cry of a corncrake, and the next thing Tommy knew, he was waking up in his bed with a lump on his head and a blackened eye. And every time he even thought of Aisling, he felt compelled to cry out like a corncrake. All the young men on the island have had the eyes for her, but none would ever dare come near her. Except for Murray, you know. He takes care of her."

"People actually believe that story?"

The barman shrugged. "They say she's a shape-shifter."

Ryan rubbed his forehead with both hands. He should never have offered this man money for such a stream of gibberish.

"What's a corncrake?" he asked, in spite of himself.

"Bird that nests here in the spring and summer, almost extinct from folks mowing over its breedin' nests. Heard more often than it's seen, at night and early in the mornin'."

Ryan drank the rest of his beer, thinking of Aisling's easy affection, her backwards lifestyle. He'd never met anyone like her. Perhaps there *was* something developmentally amiss with her, he thought, something that caused her to fabricate stories, like a child. To live in a fantasy world of myth and folklore.

"You comin' to the pub tonight?" Donal asked.

Ryan couldn't think past the DNA samples waiting for him in the West Village later in the day. "I hadn't planned on it."

"If you do happen to come around, wear this." He reached into a box near the cash register and produced a cheap rubber mask of a green-faced goblin with warts and yellow teeth. "Everyone sports a costume, and no one utters a word until midnight. It's a grand time. A pub tradition!"

"That sounds...thanks." Ryan fingered the ugly mask, thinking to himself that he'd likely spend the evening catching up with his studies.

Ryan walked from the dark pub into the warm daylight, squinting with sudden blindness. The scarecrow of a man that had poked his head into the pub earlier was lingering on the side of the stone building. When he caught sight of Ryan, he scampered around to the back of the pub.

Ryan, dazed from the beer breakfast and unusual conversation, stumbled into a pothole and dropped the mask. Face-up, the mask gaped at him, and Ryan shivered with the feeling that he was looking at his own face, transformed into its true appearance on this peculiar island.

9

———

Aisling set the buckets of water down on the dirt floor. Sweat trickled down her lower back, and her hair, giving off occasional puffs of rosemary, was almost dry. She dipped a clean barrel into the bucket and drank the cool water.

Then she smiled; while she'd been gone, Cleona had fallen asleep in her chair, mouth open and head cocked sideways. Aisling barely ran a finger over her warped knuckle and stepped into the kitchen to make the colcannon, a seasonal dish to share with Ryan Abernathy.

She reached for a pot, hung by a hook on the stone of the cottage. She imagined herself cooking for Ryan for the rest of her life, and she blushed at herself. Her mind wanted to rush ahead, to make up a story, but she held herself back. She scooped some water from a bucket into the pot, then hung it over the fire to boil.

She pulled out a few potatoes from a basket and placed them on the table. She wondered how the conversation would go, as the potatoes, boiled to a buttery softness, were eaten. Would he tell her a little about himself? What would *she* tell him, to keep him close?

As she picked up the first potato to peel, she heard a great crash; she turned to see Cleona's motionless body sprawled awkwardly on the floor. She cried out and ran to crouch beside her. Cleona's eyelids had parted slightly, but the eyes inside were colorless.

"*Mamo?*" She bent closer to her face, but felt no breath from her nose. Her body was silent as a stone, the woman inside already gone.

Aisling scampered to the front door and peered out, her eyes blurry with tears, but she saw no one on the road. She pulled hard at her hair and moaned.

The doctor had told her to expect Cleona's death in a matter of weeks, but she hadn't believed him. It was almost impossible to imagine such a long life finally coming to an end—to imagine the stream of words, the old island memories, vanish into the air, as if they'd never been.

She leaned her forehead into the door frame, then banged her head against it once, twice, three times.

Then she turned, not daring to look directly at Cleona, belly to the floor. In her line of vision was the empty chair, facing the window. Cleona had died on her favorite day of the year, she realized. She'd died while gazing out the window at the fields as they slowly took color, and beyond them, the shifting blue of the ocean.

She'd planned it that way, thought Aisling. *She'd dressed herself in her favorite outfit and waited until I'd left the cottage.*

The entire property—the land, the barn, the view of the sea

—was Cleona, and now, it all looked foreign, a bit evil. She'd never felt lost in her own home before. The alien room watched her now, wondering what she was going to do.

"I don't know," she said, then stepped to Cleona.

She carefully rolled the body over and placed Cleona's hands atop her chest. She reached out and grabbed one of the hands, still warm. The gnarled hands had guided Aisling's own small ones when Cleona had taught her how to knit; when she closed her eyes, she could still feel the heat of them, moving with surety and love. Skeins of wool still rested in a basket beside Cleona's bed, for knitting was something she could still do, despite her waning eyesight. In her last months, however, the wool had gathered dust.

Aisling stared at the earthen floor. Her mind was strangely silent, as if she too had died. Had her heart stopped beating as well? She put a hand to her chest. It was still beating, faintly, but was she forcing her lungs to take in air? Breathing no longer came naturally, she found.

She bent over and rested her head on Cleona's belly. She felt the wool of the vest prickle her forehead. She lay like that for a long while, listening to the scrubbing of the ocean against the cliffs. Then she sat up and kissed the dead woman's soft cheek. She stood up, feeling purposeful, but found that she was unsure what to do. She sat down at the table, where the potatoes and knife still rested, waiting for her to prepare a meal that was never to be eaten.

The flames of the lamps titled toward her, turning blue, then orange again. Time stalled, for a moment, suspended between seasons, lingering in the space between life and death. She wasn't ready for the darkness. She wanted only to move, to feel her heart pushing her blood through her body. Not the usual walking, the mindful plodding of one foot in front of the other. No, she wanted the recklessness of running, so that she could feel her blood torching, her lungs emptying and filling. Then she wouldn't feel the loss of Cleona quite so badly.

The brightness of the day shocked her when she emerged from the cottage. Her eyes watered a bit as she began to run as fast as she could down the low road by the beaches. Her thighs burned in the denim as she ran, panicking rabbits and startling seabirds. The ruins, the graveyard, the pockets of white sand were blurs to her. She focused on her body, its energy and force. She didn't slow until she reached the harbor. She wanted to keep running, but the island wasn't long enough. She'd have to backtrack, but the thought of running back the way she came seemed unthinkable.

She stood near the pier and tried to catch her breath. Her legs stuck to the insides of her jeans, and her sweater acted as a kind of pot-oven. It was warm as a summer day, she thought, and there wasn't any wind. *It's not natural.*

It was a day of death.

She had to tell somebody about Cleona. She couldn't just leave her there, she thought. She could tell Murray, of course. But he was out fishing today. She could tell Catherine. She *should* tell her, but she doubted the woman would know, or even care, what she was talking about.

She walked to the front door of the hotel, something she'd never done. She pushed open the door and walked inside, noting immediately the scent of bacon. She heard vague conversation in a room toward the back of the hotel.

She stood in the parlor for several minutes, unaware of

herself at all. It was as if she'd become a ghost, and was doomed to watch others live out their lives.

A door opened and Mrs. O'Sullivan bustled out with a pitcher. She set it on the sideboard, but as she made to go back through the door, she suddenly turned, her hands out in front of her, warding off trouble.

"Goodness mercy!" she cried. She lowered her hands. "Aisling...is it you?"

She swallowed hard. "I...I'm looking for Ryan Abernathy. I've something to tell him. That will help him with his work."

"Oh," she said, straightening up. "He got up very early this mornin' so he did, and I haven't seen him since. Took a map with him." She paused and stepped a bit closer to Aisling. "Is everything alright, girl? Your color's a bit off."

Aisling nodded. *Mrs. O'Sullivan really did mean well*, she thought. She thought of telling her about Cleona, but the truth was lying dead and cold, deep inside her, and refused to be brought to the light.

"Thank you," Aisling whispered, and backed out of the hotel. She gazed about the island once again, but nothing looked familiar to her. She decided to take the high road back to the West Village. Her legs creaked left-right like wooden pegs; her neck hung like a lamed goose's. She heard footsteps in front of her on the road, but couldn't bring herself to raise her head.

"Whoa!" said a man. "You might want to watch where you're going, miss!"

Something in his voice caused her to look up. The brightness of the day shocked her. She saw that it was Ryan, but he was covered in a scrim of unfamiliarity. Yet as she took in his face, a tingling sense of relief crawled from her toes to her knees.

"What is it?" he asked, stepping close to her as he shoved something dark and rubbery into his pack. His voice was low, tender.

She could hardly breathe, as the buried words shoved their way to the surface. "Cleona...Cleona is dead. I found her, when I got back."

He inhaled sharply, as if he'd known and loved Cleona for a long time. He reached out, all elbows, and embraced her lightly.

"I'm so sorry." He thumped her back.

Despite the awkwardness, she closed her eyes, feeling the barest tickle of his shirt on her cheek. She saw the pulse in his white neck, could feel his ribcage beneath her hands. Then she caught a whiff of fresh beer on his breath, and she forced herself to move away from him.

He seemed to struggle with his next words. "Are you sure she's...really passed?"

"Of course I am," she said. "You don't need to be a smart American to know when someone has died."

She began to walk down the road again. Aisling's tears still hadn't flowed; she could feel the backup, an aching in her sinuses.

"Where are you going?" he asked from behind. "What...what are you planning on doing?"

"I don't know," she said. She wiped the sweat from her cheeks with hot hands.

He nodded as if he understood and continued to follow at her side.

They passed the old graveyard—a mess of stones, weeds and wildflowers—and her mind suddenly filled with thoughts of Cleona. With every step, she turned over a new memory, and her heart strained with the effort of acknowledgment.

The words finally came then. "Her life was dull, full of hard work and heartache, but she had imagination. She told me stories every night, no matter how old I became. She knew thousands of stories of all kinds, and a long time ago, people would gather at her hearth to listen."

"So she was like a professional storyteller?" Ryan asked.

Aisling barely nodded. "But as she grew older and even older, she stopped tellin' stories. She told me they were still there, but locked inside her, and she couldn't find the key."

The absence of stories had gouged a crater in Aisling's life, for she no longer heard about her mother and father, her ancestors. The stories had stretched all the way to the beginning, and gave Aisling a sense of place in the world.

Work had dominated their lives together, so that personal conversation was brief, unimportant. But when Cleona told stories, at night when the work was done, it allowed Aisling to peek inside the old woman's mind to see the wild imagination, the spectrum of her loneliness and sadness but also her moments of joy and satisfaction. She had learned about Cleona's entire life through the countless stories, and in this way, Aisling had learned how to love someone.

"Now the stories are yours," he said.

"Aye," she said, realizing that he was right. Cleona had planned that too.

She saw that he wore a watch on his wrist, a big black device that told him the time every moment of the day. He seemed to be a person who wanted answers, orderly facts. She stopped walking and turned to face him.

"I wanted to tell you, for your work," she said, taking a deep breath. "Cleona was 180 years old."

Ryan stared at her, his big brown eyes huge behind his glasses. His lips wiggled like two worms. "I...I don't think that's possible. Whatever she told you, those stories, it's not---"

"It's in our blood. Many generations, on this island."

He stared at her. She could almost hear the needles of his mind clicking. "Do you have proof of that?"

"No," she answered.

"Again, Aisling, Stories aren't very scientific. I'd need a birth certificate or a baptism record, something official."

"She was born on this island in 1842. I don't know a thing about records."

She could see that his eyes, once kind and concerned, were now full of doubt. "Born in 1842," he repeated. "That's just...I'm sorry to be so blunt, especially after your loss, but it's simply not possible."

Her voice trembled. "In a line of such long lives, it's not so far-fetched."

Ryan nodded, but his eyes formed narrow slits. "But that age..."

"Cleona and Catherine are unusual."

"Yes, I guess they are."

"You don't believe me."

"I don't," he said softly.

In his world of big books and research studies, he would never understand. She saw that now, but she couldn't think what to say to change his mind. She began to sob, but still the tears refused to flow.

He put a tentative hand on her knee. "I think you've had a shock today. I think living on this island—away from normal civilization and people your own age—has confused you and... you're a bit out of touch with reality."

She shook her head fiercely. She had to tell Catherine about her sister's death, had a wake to plan, a funeral. She forced herself down the road again, and still Ryan walked beside her. They continued on until they reached Catherine's cottage; she imagined, in the house right next door, that Cleona still lay stiffly on the floor, the heat from the fever slowly cooling. Suddenly, she didn't want Ryan to leave her here.

"You could still meet Catherine." She added, "She's grown older than Cleona, now."

Ryan opened his mouth to say something, but quickly closed it. He bent close to her and kissed her, lightly, on the cheek.

"I'm so sorry," he murmured, and she felt his breath tickle the skin of her neck. The faint scent of lavender embraced her as she watched him walk away.

10

———

Ryan hated cemeteries, grassy ground full of dead, decaying bodies. It was macabre, dressing up the dead and sticking them in satin-lined boxes, then driving the boxes to the cemetery in a black station wagon with pulled polyester curtains.

As a little game, his childhood friends used to hold their breaths when they drove past a cemetery. Once safely past the rows and rows of plastic flowers and slabs of marble, they'd let their breaths out in a collective whoosh.

Already acquainted with death at that point, Ryan didn't play the game; he breathed and breathed until he would almost hyperventilate.

They would chant,

Don't ever laugh when a hearse goes by, or you may be the next to die.
They wrap you up in a bloody sheet, and bury you under about six feet.

*All goes well for a couple of weeks, but then your coffin
begins to leak.
The worms crawl in, the worms crawl out, the worms play
pinochle on your snout.
Your stomach turns a slimy green, and puss comes out of
you like whipped cream. You lap it up with a piece of
bread, and that's what you eat when you are dead.*

Ryan would hold his ears and hum loudly until their laughter subsided.

Cemeteries held no pull over him; they only reminded him of his paucity of belief. The so-called souls of his mother, father and brother weren't in the ground, he knew. He didn't believe in souls, and he didn't believe in heaven or God, waiting for the believers to arrive at the holy gates. He believed in worms. He believed in bones. He didn't believe in anything that he couldn't logically deduce.

So it surprised him when he found himself walking up the hill, no trace of tightness in his chest. He took in evenly spaced breaths of the clean air, and thought of Aisling's face, dripping sweat, as if the loss was manifesting itself in perspiration. He had tried his best to comfort her, despite her obvious precariousness. Grief, he knew, had a way of wringing the cloth of personality into a twisted, bitter rag.

He couldn't believe Cleona was really gone. *One hundred-eighty years old*, he thought, his mind expanding to consider the possibility. *It was absurd*, he told himself. *Wasn't it?*

From the top of the graveyard, the gravestones spread down the hill in a chaotic calamity, but the view of the rocky hills and lake was breathtaking. The ocean flattened itself to the horizon, not far from where he stood. The spot suggested eternity, unlike most of the manicured golf course-cemeteries found in America.

Tall weeds and grass grew wildly over the stone slabs and Celtic crosses, often obscuring the names of the buried. He parted some of the grass growing against one of the older looking ones. It bore the inscription: *James O'Flaherty, 1872-1930. Father, husband, brother, one with the sea.*

He passed among several other tombstones; some were newer, with clean lines and cross-shaped boxes full of dirty plastic flowers adorning them, and some were older, covered with moss and clearly forgotten.

A couple with the surname of McNally, a few with the surname of Connolly and Fitzgerald and Finnegan. After a few minutes of searching, he found a small, rectangular gravestone with the name Owen. *Orla Owen, 1943-1997.* He thought of the barman's story, and considered whether Aisling's mother, who had perished in childbirth, was buried beneath his feet. He'd never heard of a woman having a baby at the age of 54, unless it was scientifically orchestrated.

More intrigued, he moved to a similar stone next to it. It read *Michael Owen, fisherman, husband, father.* This was Aisling's father, who had died in a bad storm at sea at the age of 58, in 2000.

He moved to the next stone, but it wasn't an *Owen.* He searched through the next set of stones for several more minutes, but with no luck. Happy to have found Aisling's mother and father, he decided to head back to the hotel.

But as he walked through the grassy meadow to reach the low road, he tripped over something hidden in the grass. He crouched, parting the grass with his hands, and saw an old stone, dark grey and split almost in two. It appeared to have once had carvings, for he could see faint marks on the surface.

He straightened up and scanned the meadow for more possible hidden stones, but could see nothing obvious. So he began crawling through the thick, yellow meadow, hoping that no one happened by on the low road.

After a few moments of careful searching, he found another stone, dark green and cracked down the center. He cleaned his glasses of dirt and dust with his shirttail and bent close to the stone. He saw an O, and he traced his finger over the four lost letters. Yes, it appeared that this was an *Owen,* but the first name had been lost to time. He brushed away some dirt and weeds that covered the bottom of the marker. The dates, although worn in places, seemed to read *1542-1688.*

He ran his fingers over the numbers, as carefully as if he were reading Braille.

"My God," he said. He looked away, the blood zinging in his ears so loudly that he couldn't hear the gulls directly overhead.

To be fair, the first "8" could possibly have been a "5." It was almost impossible to tell which it was. If the dates were what he thought they were, the person had lived for either 146 years or 116 years. *If* he could trust the marker, the person buried in the plot below had been a super-centenarian—110-years-old or older —and he or she had achieved this milestone during a time of famine, plague and poor hygiene. In the sixteenth and seventeenth centuries, the average life expectancy was around 35 to 40 years.

He laughed out loud. Hadn't anyone on the island seen this stone before? Hadn't any tourists stumbled across it while roaming about the fields, chasing birds? Surely it would have been publicized by now, ridiculed on the internet and discussed by news media.

Maybe the carvings weren't even accurate, he thought. The stone-cutter had made a mistake in his math, or had perhaps been illiterate. Or had listened to a confused family member.

Even so, Ryan spent the next two hours crawling around the cemetery like a hungry wolf. He examined each and every hidden stone in the meadow, yet most of the carvings were completely worn away by the rains and wind. There were dozens of them.

∞

Still sitting in the cemetery, Ryan pulled out his cell phone and called Rose Buxton, five hours back in the States.

"Hello?" she answered groggily.

"Hi Rose, it's Ryan."

"Ryan!" She coughed a couple of times, clearing her throat. "We haven't heard a thing from you since you left! Tell me everything!"

"Listen, Rose, I've got a question for you."

"Oh." She sounded disappointed. "Wakes me from the most delicious dream and then won't even tell me about his—"

"Say that I want to find out how old a body is," he interrupted. "How would I go about doing that?"

She took a couple of seconds for her to respond. "Whose body? Is it dead or alive?"

"A skeleton."

She huffed. "Ryan, what on earth? Why are you asking such a question?"

"Look, I'm in a cemetery that appears to contain a very long-lived dead person."

"Really?" she asked. "*How* long? Like, super-centenarian long?"

"Yes. That long."

"Wow!" She paused. "You're in a cemetery on Halloween?"

Ryan ignored her. "You're a pathologist, right? Isn't there a way to figure out exactly how old the bones are?"

"I'm *studying* to be a pathologist."

"Come on, Rose."

"Well, there is a way, of course. It's a bit tedious, though."

"Go on..."

"Are you sure you have the time to listen? I mean, you sound a little rushed."

"Rose!"

"Okay, okay. It's called the Kerley method. The pathologist slices off a wafer-thin cross section of a long bone, such as a femur. The cross-section reveals circular canals, or osteons, that carry blood and nourishment through the bone. Good so far?"

"Osteons, yes! Go on!"

"Well, concentric circles form around the osteons, like the age rings of a tree. The older a person gets, the more fragmented the osteons become. The pathologist compares the number of healthy osteons to the fragmented older ones and applies them to a math equation. Ta-da! The age at death can be calculated pretty reliably."

He ran a hand over the old tombstone. "Rose, could you do that for me? On one of the bones from this cemetery?"

"What?" she barked. "Are you insane?"

"A little bit, yes," he admitted, blinking in the light that shone off the lake near the cemetery. "I need confirmation of the dates on these tombstones. I would never forgive myself if I left this island, having seen this, without knowing the truth."

He could hear Rose's parrot Louie squawking in the drawn-out silence. She finally said, "It's doable."

"How long will it take?"

"I don't know. I've never done the test before," she said. "You should really wait for my dad to help with this, Ryan. He could fly out, check out the stone himself."

Ryan groaned. "Too much red tape," he said. "He'll want to notify the Irish authorities and everything. You know your dad. I want to do this now. Myself."

Rose was quiet for a few moments. "Have you thought about what you're saying? You'll need to get a bone from the grave."

"I know."

"You'll have to actually dig up the ground and open the coffin and---!"

"I know."

"And I'll have to sneak around the lab, and use equipment I'm not authorized to use," she moaned. "And I know that it's very time-consuming. It's used mostly on old mummies, stuff like that. Only in unusual circumstances."

"This *is* unusual."

She exhaled loudly. "Did you even speak with the women yet?"

"No...I haven't," he said. "Rose, one of the women died today. Cleona Owen."

"No," she groaned. "She was the one with pneumonia, right?"

"That's right. She looked biblically ancient. I've never seen anyone quite like her in my life."

"Guess you can't request a cheek swab from her now, huh?"

"That, and there's no documentation in sight," he sighed. "You wouldn't believe how these women live! They don't use electricity or indoor plumbing! It's really backwards."

"You could still get a sample from Catherine though, right?"

"I'll try to, after the funeral," he said. It would be hard to wait, he knew. "Rose, I'm going to go now. I'll try to mail the bone to you."

"I'll be on the lookout for a long, skinny box."

"Thanks Rose. This means a great deal to me. You know that, right?"

"Yes, I'll bet it does."

"Don't tell your dad, okay? Don't tell anyone."

She paused. "Are you okay, Ryan?"

He bit his lip. "Not really."

"You taking your meds?"

He almost said he was, until he realized that he hadn't taken his anti-anxiety medication, nor any vitamins or supplements, since yesterday morning.

∞

Ireland, Ryan learned, was one of the hardest countries in Europe in which to trace ancestors. In Ireland, the civil registration of births, marriages, and deaths only began in 1864. Before this, church registers had the only reference to such data, but because of the destruction by fire of many Church of Ireland burial records in 1922, and the late beginning dates of many

Roman Catholic and Presbyterian burial registers, a gravestone inscription could be the only record of an ancestor's life and death.

And even then, he thought, *the names might be lost to time.*

Moreover, Cleona and Catherine would not have been issued birth certificates, *if* they'd been born in 1842. He chuckled aloud at the thought. Most of the nineteenth century census records had been lost; even if the sisters and their family members appeared in the surviving 1901 and 1911 censuses or the later twentieth century censuses, it was possible that ages were reported wrong or written inaccurately.

He closed his laptop roughly and rubbed his eyes with both fists. He admitted to himself that there was no easy way to verify the women's ages. A search for them in the Public Records Office or the Genealogical Office would likely require a trip to Dublin and long weeks of record-searching, which might, in the end, prove fruitless.

He gazed about him at the empty cubicles of the island's community center, wondering who would lock the building when he left. Perhaps it was left unlocked, for there was nothing to steal except a vending machine and a rack of soccer balls in the gym.

It was already 10:30 p.m., but he decided to venture to the pub. He figured that it was too early to visit the cemetery on Halloween night, and he couldn't abide the stack of textbooks in his hotel room.

At the door to the pub, he pulled his mask on, careful to avoid crushing his glasses. And just as Donal had suggested, the pub was completely silent. He opened the door to see that the poorly lit room was packed with costumed people. Faces were concealed behind masks, and everyone was quietly drinking.

Ryan watched as a ghoul at the bar wrote something down on a small piece of paper and handed it to the barman. Donal, dressed as a Druid with a blue mask and a long white tunic, poured a glass of whiskey and bowed deeply as he handed it over.

Ryan sidled through the crowd and wrote "beer" on a piece of paper with a stubby pencil. Donal nodded wisely and poured him a glass of dark beer from the tap. Then he wrote something else on Ryan's piece of paper and placed the beer on top of it.

Ryan lifted the beer to retrieve the paper. On it was written "*watch your back.*"

Chest squeezing, Ryan turned to look at the fiendish faces all around him. Then he crumpled the paper in a sweaty hand and stuffed it into the pocket of his jeans. He reminded himself that he too was wearing a mask.

Moving the goblin face hardly two inches up, he forced himself to drink the warm beer quickly. Then he moved to the rear of the pub slowly, passing through devils and dragons, ninjas and skeletons and popes. With his back to the wall, he watched the silent islanders, mostly men from what he could tell. His glass soon was empty, but he couldn't make himself go back to the bar. *It was ridiculous to be afraid,* he told himself. He probably should just go back to the hotel.

Just as he turned for the door, a man dressed as an armored warrior walked up to him, and without fanfare, pulled him by the upper arm through the sea of silent pub-goers. He directed Ryan to an open door in the back of the pub and pushed him through it. In the darkness outside were two other men, one wearing the mask of a rotting corpse and the other wearing an old bedsheet printed with rabbits and chicks. The ghost's two eyes stared from roughly cut holes in the thin sheet, and a large gaping slash allowed access to the mouth, already wet with drink.

Next to the ghost, the fists of the dead man clenched. Ryan had seen those angry, sea-cut hands before. Murray cocked his mask back on his face and took a long draught.

"You're not very good at blending in, are you?" he asked. "Spotted your shiny, white trainers a mile away."

"What do you want with me?" said Ryan. He noted a vague scent of stale piss, emanating from beneath his feet.

"Why are you still on my island?" asked Murray, his voice warped from behind the corpse mask.

"I'm conducting research."

Donal's glaring, blue face appeared in the doorway. "Don't you boys think of startin' any trouble now," he warned.

"Leave off, Donal, and tend to your pub," said Murray. "We won't be long."

Donal stood in the doorway for another long moment, then bustled back into the pub, his cape swooping behind him.

Ryan removed his mask, grateful for the rush of air on his face. "I'm a geneticist. I'm not looking for trouble."

Murray moved so that he was less than an inch from Ryan's face. "Wankers like you have been comin' to the island since I was nothing but a lad. Wantin' to buy our land, our houses, and tear 'em down to build new ones for their bloody holidays! You knock about in your slick clothin', thinkin' you own us. But sure you're off your nut, sniffin' around Aisling like you are."

"I'm not interested in Aisling," Ryan whispered. "And I don't want your land or your house. I came to speak with Cleona and Catherine about their ages. I'd like to study their DNA."

It really had been that simple, Ryan realized with a shock.

Murray pounded his fist on the concrete of the pub. "It was your pesterin' that popped her granny's clogs," he shouted. "The poor woman couldn't take the shock of you."

"She died of pneumonia," said Ryan. "She died before I even got a DNA sample from her."

The other men's feet shifted anxiously on the gravel.

"Everything out of your mouth sounds like a bloody load of bullocks to me," said Murray. "D and A doesn't have a thing to do with us. And I'd wonder greatly on the manhood of a man who doesn't have the eyes for Aisling!"

The other men snickered. Ryan could feel the heat from their bodies, they were so close to him.

Merry shouts suddenly made their way to them from the inside of the pub. Ryan guessed that it was midnight, but didn't have the courage to glance at his watch. His backpack pulled at his shoulders like a wild animal.

Again Donal appeared in the doorway. He held a violin. "Stop toyin' round with the tourist, Murray Finnegan!" he said. "Cut us a tune for once."

"A minute more, Donal," said Murray.

"No, no," said Donal, stepping over to hand Murray the violin. "Sure but the men are already foamin' at the mouth for some music. Come on now."

Murray leaned in close to Ryan. "Are you going to leave us alone, Yank?" he whispered. "Catch the ferry tomorrow mornin', bright and early?"

The noise of the crowd encouraged a recklessness he'd never felt before. "I'm not leaving this island," Ryan whispered back. "Until I get what I came for."

Murray reached out with both hands and pushed Ryan hard into the concrete wall of the pub, causing him to drop the rubber mask to the ground. But Donal reached a strong hand between them.

"Stop it now! Come inside the pub," he pleaded.

When Murray's hand reluctantly released Ryan's chest, Ryan took the chance to dart away from the group and sprint into the night, but his hips felt rusty with the exertion of running, and his pack weighed him down. From behind, he heard Donal yelling.

As he ran, he recalled that Aisling had said that Murray had a "long stride," and it was then that he felt something hard smash into his head, heard the garish twang of a fiddle deep in his head. He grabbed for his glasses, but they had already flown off his face. An invisible fist landed on his nose, then someone strong hurled him to the ground.

Something hot dripped thickly down the back of his throat, and as he put his hand to his nose, a booted foot cocked him in the cheek. He cried out with the newest flood of pain. Before he could do anything, though, the boot kicked him hard in the stomach, and he doubled in two. Then someone picked him up by the shirt and punched him in his mouth. His lip split.

He began to lose consciousness.

"Maybe now she won't think you're so fine," said Murray. Ryan heard a hunk of spit land next to his face.

"Didn't take much to knock him out," said another. "The scrawny ass that he is."

Ryan smelled alcohol on breath. "Hump off, Yank."

He felt hands grab his arms and legs and carry him to another spot, further off the road. Then, in a thick fog, he heard them walk away, plucking the broken fiddle and laughing. He drifted for a long time, aware that he was swallowing his own blood but unable to do anything about it. He wanted to get up, but he felt trapped, as if in a coffin. He didn't want to die.

He couldn't see his mother, or his father, or his brother, or his grandparents. He was surprised when he saw Harriet, the tortoise who had died in 2006 at the age of 175; she crawled out of the darkness to assess his injuries. She told him—in an Australian accent—that he'd have some bruises and possibly a broken nose, but nothing remotely serious.

She told him to focus on the problem at hand. It was most important that he keep the people away from the Galapagos Islands, for their feral dogs, cats, pigs and black rats were ravaging the nests and young tortoises. The donkeys, cattle and horses were grazing on their land, depleting their food sources. Foreigners were taking the tortoises away from the island to study them, and she said that she didn't want to end up in a museum or a zoo, with people rubbing her shell and watching her all day.

He told her that he'd certainly try to help her, but humans were a stubborn, selfish lot. He doubted there was much he could do.

11

———————

He felt his glasses being slid along the sides of his heavy head. He opened his eyes and saw an elderly person in a nun costume looming over him through cracked and crooked lenses.

He tried to breathe, but his nostrils were clogged. He touched the tip of his nose gingerly and gasped in pain. He felt the blood on his cheek as he ran a tentative hand over the swell of his cheekbone.

The skin of the nun's face matched the white veil next to it. She put a hand to his face, left it there for a few moments. Then she stood up, crossed herself, and in an instant, she was gone, her footsteps barely making a sound on the gravel.

He tried to call out to her, but his mouth wouldn't open.

Ryan closed his eyes and tried to remember. As the details of the roadside ambush came back to him, he remained immobile for several long minutes, assessing his strength, gathering his breath. Growing up, he'd never had many friends, either male or female. Some had called him shy, for he'd been too good-looking to be termed a "nerd." He'd been studious, reserved. But he'd never once been punched.

He thought of Aisling, mourning the death of Cleona in the tiny, backwards cottage. He had to be strong on this island.

He opened his eyes and pulled his glasses from his throbbing face; the lens on the right side was damaged beyond repair, so he poked the shards from the frame and put the glasses back on. His distance vision was compromised, but he would manage. He slowly got to his feet and adjusted his pack. He began to wobble toward the hotel.

Around the back, he found the shed that he'd remembered seeing upon his arrival. The door squeaked when he pulled it open, and the smell of dried dirt and old grass greeted him. He fished around in his pack for his little flashlight, which he clicked on before he stepped further inside.

Amidst clay pots, rubber hose, and rakes and hoes of all varieties, he soon located a large shovel. He then searched on a wall rack for a crowbar.

His labored breathing echoed off the dank walls of the shed. He felt monstrous, the goblin come alive. His mind rattled loudly, as if Murray had knocked something free inside, something gossamer and previously inaccessible—giddy anger, abysmal grief.

He was the man that he'd been afraid of becoming, he supposed. The man who had been denied.

This man now had tools. He walked in the light of the moon to the low road along the beaches. There was no sound; not even the seabirds were awake. There was a faint aroma of burned wood in the air, likely from a recent bonfire.

He soon saw the tombstones, leaning crookedly like drunks

over a pint. It was completely silent at the top of the hill, with just a hint of wind to stir the grasses. The island's Halloween celebrations were over.

He gripped the tools tightly in both hands and walked slowly through the meadow. He felt around with his feet, then put the tools down and shone the flashlight over the stones. He looked them over again, not stopping until he came to the anonymous marker with the carved dates. He looked about him once more, to be sure he was alone, and began digging in the space around the marker. The soil was fairly rocky, so he threw his back into the exercise.

After a few minutes, he stood up to stretch his back, and for half a second, he saw himself for what he was—a grave-robbing geneticist. There was no denying the illegality of what he was doing, yet he didn't throw down the shovel, disgusted with himself. He giggled at the digging man; he was *proud* of him, for pulling what he wanted from the rocky ground of death. He set again to the task.

As his head spun and pounded, he scooped and shoveled in the darkness for what seemed like a long time, constantly wondering if he was digging in the wrong place. His nose bled down his chin and neck, wetting his shirt, and he hardly noticed the fluids clogging his nostrils. He dug several feet into the ground before his shovel turned over some stubborn rocks.

In frustration, he climbed down into the space he'd made, and after shining the flashlight, he found himself standing not among rocks but in a pit of bones. There was no coffin after all— it was a pauper's grave.

A sort of smile spread over his face, cracking some of the dried blood on his cheeks.

As he stooped to examine the bones in the white light of the flashlight, he heard the youthful brashness of teens, one male and one female. It sounded as if they were walking down the hill from the high road, and moving closer with every second. Ryan clicked off the flashlight and huddled into the hole, trying to breath quietly through his mouth.

He heard the male voice say, "Watch out for the ghouls, now, girl. This bone yard is full of old spirits."

"If you're tryin' to scare me, it's workin'," said the female, even closer. "Mam won't even let me near here, superstitious old goat."

Ryan caught a strong scent of burned wood from them. In silence, he began to inspect the findings. The skull, with its open mouth and elongated teeth, seemed happy to be found almost five centuries later. Scraps of damp, dirty cloth still clung to what looked like the ribs.

The boy said, "I once saw a ghost in this very cemetery, you know. Have I told you that story?"

"Aye, Seamus. A thousand times." She exhaled as she sat down. "'Twas the ghost of your ancestor that died in the famine. Skinny and dirty and mad as a wet hen."

He laughed. "Maybe we'll see him tonight. We'll have to be patient, now."

"What'll we do with all the time?" joked the girl.

Ryan heard the sound of lips meeting, of hands on clothes.

In the hole, he ran his raw hands over his facial injuries. The drying blood lay as thickly as icing on his face, and his nose and cheekbone were badly swollen, he knew. His clothing was smeared with blood and dirt. He had no idea what time it was, but he knew the dawn would come more quickly than he'd like.

He placed his glasses in his jacket pocket, and using his hands and fingers, he clawed his way from the hole. He stood up and with the moonlight in his eyes, saw the vague outlines of two people sitting nearby on the hill. The boy appeared to be dressed in some kind of a costume and the girl wore a witch hat.

Ryan groaned and held his arms out in front of him, and the couple turned to face him. And for a moment, he felt just as a zombie might feel. He had no thoughts, especially no guilt or fear. He was aware of a burning desire though, certainly not the flesh of living humans, but his desire compelled him to scare, to intimidate at all costs.

"Jesus, Mary and Joseph!" screeched the girl. She scrambled up and without a backward glance began running back up the hill.

"What the...?" said the boy, as he stared in horror at the creature in front of him. "Seamus, is it you?"

Ryan bobbed his head up and down, a slow, broken movement of his neck.

The boy crossed himself slowly. "Can I help you, Seamus? Get you something?" he asked, his voice trembling.

"Come...closer," Ryan moaned. "I'm starvin'!"

The boy gasped and sprinted up the hill, periodically looking back at Ryan as he ran. Ryan watched, and groaned, as the two of them disappeared into the darkness.

Quickly, he jumped back into the hole and felt among the bones, finally finding one of the longer ones. He pulled it from the jumble, held it up to the moon and decided that it was a femur bone, darkened with age and the elements.

Frenzied, he climbed out of the hole with the bone and began covering the skeleton with dirt. He smoothed the mess as best as he could with the shovel and tossed some small rocks and clumps of long grass atop it. Then he ran back to the low road, the bone, shovel and crowbar clanking with every other stride.

∞

Bones weren't meant to be buried forever, he told himself as he ran. Bones were potential DNA samples, and were meant to be studied, so that future generations could learn from them.

When Ryan was 13 or 14 and living with his grandparents, he had taken a great interest in archaeology after reading an article about Egyptian mummies in a nature magazine. The article was accompanied by graphic pictures of King Tut's embalmed body and gilded wooden sarcophagus, as well as his richly appointed burial chamber. He lost himself for weeks in what was left of the 3,300-year-old boy king.

As eviscerated as he had appeared, Tut hadn't disintegrated to dust. He was still on the earth, and looked sort of human. He still lived—the goal of the ancient Egyptians realized, in a way.

Egyptians believed in life after death, and to Ryan, mummies possessed a definite immortality. The search for lost worlds and reincarnated lives intrigued him deeply. There on his grandmother's afghan-covered sofa, he had decided to become an archaeologist; during his first two years of college, he worked to that aim, following the study of the Egyptian mummies, especially when the DNA testing of the royal mummies began. This testing endeavored to construct the definitive chronology of Egyptian kings by matching the DNA of supposedly royal mummies and mummified fetuses with the DNA of known mummies.

Ryan had been fascinated to learn that DNA alone could illuminate such history. Archaeology had begun the investigations, but genetics could now solve the mystery of a mummy's ancestry—who he was and to whom he was related.

DNA testing, he realized, could be applied to any ancient skeleton. Yes, clothing would thin, metals would rust, skin would rot, but DNA was always there, waiting to tell its stories. *It allowed the dead to speak.* To Ryan, this science had seemed more important—more suggestive of immortality—and his focus had soon shifted to the study of genetics, biochemistry and the future of DNA.

He hadn't looked back, until tonight.

What I've done tonight was no more serious than an archaeological dig, but without the necessary red tape, he thought. *I'm solving a mystery, just like Howard Carter, when he discovered King Tut's tomb.*

Carter had descended into a darkened tomb, and come out enlightened. *The same could happen here, on this island,* he thought.

∞

Back in his hotel room, he wrapped the bone in a white bath towel and packaged it in a discarded box he found in the back of the empty pub. He shoved it into the closet.

His mind buzzing as if full of disturbed wasps, he showered, watching the dirt and blood darken the water in pools around his feet. He cleaned his wounds as best as he could without looking at them too closely. His nose might be broken, but his face looked a bit better without the layer of bloody grit.

He dressed in clean clothes and crept down to the hotel's darkened dining room, hoping to find something to eat and drink besides the small package of walnuts in his backpack. His belly growled, as if he hadn't eaten in days.

But the tables were empty, with fresh tablecloths already draped across them. He walked into the front parlor, but the sideboard was empty as well. Defeated, he was about to turn for the stairs when he heard a man cough. Ryan turned quickly, his heart hammering.

"Good God, man, what happened to you?"

Ryan squinted into the lamplight in the parlor and saw the British writer, sitting in an armchair with a notebook on his lap.

Ryan put a hand to his swollen cheekbone. "Too much fun at the pub. You know how it goes."

The man laughed. "Halloween *is* traditionally a time of giving vent to one's emotions," he said, making a fist and mock-punching his own jaw. "Looks to me like the tradition is still alive and well on this island. Tell me, have you thought about contact lenses?"

Ryan reached up to touch his broken glasses. "Maybe I should."

"Name's Wally Rose," said the man. He extended a fleshy hand, and Ryan shook it.

"Ryan Abernathy. I came down looking for some food, but I can't seem to find anything around."

"Did you check the refrigerator?"

Ryan raised his eyebrows. "Well, no."

"Come on then." Wally got up and led Ryan through the door into the dark kitchen. He flipped a wall switch, shedding light on the dated, yellow appliances. Wally opened the crowded refrigerator, and they both gazed at the middle shelf, where rested a container of some kind of cake with a bowl covered in plastic wrap on top of it.

"Sticky toffee pudding!" Wally exclaimed. "Wonderful woman, Dorothy. I told her yesterday it was my favorite dessert."

He placed it on the counter, and Ryan searched the drawers for spoons. With easy hands, Wally removed the cake from the container, cut two slices from the rectangular loaf, and placed them on plates. Then he microwaved the bowl's contents and spooned the dark goo over the cake.

"Do you think Dorothy will mind?" asked Ryan, taking a plate and carving his spoon into the cake-like pudding.

Wally shook his head, then spooned a dripping bite recklessly into his mouth. "Oh, my God," he groaned. "She's a Brit at heart."

Trying, and failing, to count the mostly alcoholic calories he'd had throughout the day, Ryan followed suit. Maneuvering the spoon around his busted lip proved difficult, however, and he dropped a bit of sauce onto his shirt. But he hardly cared; it had been too long since he'd had something so delicious.

The two men ate spoonful after spoonful in comfortable silence. It seemed that the more of the pudding he ate, the better his face felt.

After a while Ryan said, "I heard you were a poet."

"And an academic of sorts. Irish literature to be exact."

"So what is your poetry about?" Ryan asked. "English desserts?"

Wally took another bite of the pudding, then swallowed mightily, his eyes closed.

"Death," he stated matter-of-factly.

The man appeared too cherubic to write about death. "Death? Just...death?" asked Ryan. His chest gave a quick squeeze. "Isn't that kind of morbid, for a pudding lover?"

"I suppose," he said, with a toffee-stained smile. He held out an arm and began to speak with theatrical verve. "*Nor dread nor hope attend a dying animal; a man awaits his end dreading and hoping all; many times he died, many times rose again. A great man in his pride, confronting murderous men, casts derision upon supersession of breath; he knows death to the bone—Man has created death.*" *Death* by William Butler Yeats, famous Irish poet."

Ryan grinned, having no idea what the bombastic words meant. "So there's something about this island that inspires your interest in the subject of death?"

Wally put his well-licked spoon on the plate. "Very much so. Have you ever seen the western side of the island do battle with a stormy sea? The island 'knows death to the bone,' I should say."

Wally sauntered back to the parlor. Ryan followed, and they sat down in the overstuffed armchairs beside the low-burning fire. The hotel was quiet, save the ticking clock on a book-laden shelf.

"The people here used to live their lives in survival mode, always one step away from death. It does me good to come here and imagine what it must have been like."

Ryan cringed inside; he would never want to purposefully imagine such a state.

"You might be interested to know that an elderly West Village woman—who appeared to live according to the old customs—passed away today," Ryan said.

"Dorothy told me this afternoon," he said. "She said the woman's twin still lives next door."

Ryan nodded. "Well, I'm here as a researcher with a longevity study. I was going to meet with the women, but the sister passed before I could get a DNA sample from her."

"How old was she, then?" he asked, his eyes round with curiosity.

"I haven't been able to get an exact age, but her great-granddaughter says..." He trailed off, trying not to dwell on Aisling's strange stories. "She says that she's over 100. But she has no official age documents."

Wally thought for a moment, his finger to his lips. "Will the twin have the same DNA?"

"Yes, they're identical twins."

"So your trip won't be a total loss, then."

"I suppose not," Ryan admitted. "But two sets of DNA could illuminate certain 'longevity' genes the two had in common. And that's really why I'm here."

Ryan stood up, suddenly exhausted, the weight of the entire night on his bony back. "I'm going to the wake tomorrow. You should come along," he said. "Could spark a good poem."

Wally sighed. "I love a good Irish wake."

12

———

Ryan's lower lip was so swollen that he was having trouble keeping saliva in his mouth. He'd been standing in line at the island post office for over an hour, carefully wiping the corner of his mouth with a tissue.

The post office was really the downstairs portion of a two-story home, similar in size and style to the hotel. Some people waited on a sunken sofa, reading magazines, but Ryan remained standing.

The three people ahead of him had each engaged in long, personal conversations with the elderly female postal worker behind a glass partition at the opposite end of the living room. Ryan gripped the big box with two cramped hands, until he was forced to put it at his feet. The greasy "bangers" and eggs that he'd eaten for breakfast turned circles in his belly. To pass the time, he counted the calories in his breakfast, and scolded himself for veering so far off his regimen.

Finally, it was his turn, and he lifted the box to the counter.

The old woman's smile, used specifically for the locals, faded when she saw a bruised tourist with broken glasses standing before her. She shoved her own steel-framed glasses closer to her nose and peered at the box.

"What do we have here?" she asked, opening the partition and reaching a hand through to pat the box.

"What do you mean?" he asked, barely able to enunciate.

"What's in the box?" she asked loudly, as if he were hard of hearing.

"Nothing," stammered Ryan. *Only an old bone dug from a graveyard on Halloween night.* "Why do you need to know?"

She shrugged. "I don't. Just wantin' to be friendly is all."

She took the box in weathered hands and weighed it on some old-fashioned scales.

"Not too heavy, for such a big box," she said accusingly.

Ryan looked past her head, into the room cluttered with packages and envelopes. A dish of cat food sat atop a nearby box. He worried, suddenly, if his package would ever make it to America. She inspected the address he had written on the outside of it.

"A bit of Ireland goin' to America, that's the way of it so it is," she said wistfully. "Who's Rose, then?"

Ryan blotted his mouth. "A friend," he said.

"That's what they all say nowadays," she scolded. "Whatever happened to courtin', is what I want to know."

Ryan paid her more euros than he believed he should have. And when he walked past the group of waiting locals, they all stared at him, even the orange-mustached child with no shoes.

Back in the morning sunlight, he took deep breaths in an effort to loosen his chest. An airplane cruised overhead, silent and alien in the thick, blue sky. He thought of honking cars, cell phone towers, skyscrapers, and crowded restaurants, as if he'd dreamed them.

∞

As he walked down the road toward the hotel, he passed another two-story home, similar to the hotel and the post office, but a hand-painted sign above the door read "Dunleavey's Market."

He saw in the window two paintings, and as he neared he saw that one of the paintings was of a small, stone cottage similar to Aisling's. Another featured waving, brown fields, stretching to the sea, the colors earthy and the moods careful, somber. He couldn't make out the signature of the artist at the bottom right of the paintings.

Ryan thought he could use some painkillers for his throbbing face, so he ventured through the market's front door, a bell tinkling his arrival.

An elderly man sat in a rocking chair near the door, next to an old-fashioned cash register. He nodded to Ryan, then continued rocking. The tiny market bore a few wire shelves with boxed cake mixes, jars of jam, drums of salt, canned fruits and vegetables, and lots of candy, and a refrigerated case contained some triangles of orange cheese and two glass bottles of milk. Ryan didn't see any painkillers.

"Do you have anything that will help with pain?" Ryan asked the old man. "Aspirin, maybe?"

The man cracked a gummy smile. "I got some poteen under the counter here."

"No, thanks, I can't drink that stuff," laughed Ryan, a hand on the door knob. "Those paintings in the window. They're beautiful."

The man turned to the canvases in the window and squinted, as if trying to figure out what Ryan was talking about.

"Aye, those were painted by Old Pat Michael Dunleavey. This was his shop, so it was. He passed on about two years ago," the man said. "He's got a few paintings here in the back, all of 'em for sale. You want to take a look?"

"Sure," said Ryan. The wake wasn't due to start for another couple of hours.

The old man took his time getting up from the chair. Then he slowly hobbled with a cane toward the back of the building. He opened a door and led Ryan into a room with many large windows. The sunlight shone directly on an easel that was still set up near one of the windows. A canvas was propped on the easel, the beginnings of the gray water of the harbor visible in the sun. Tubes of paint and a container of brushes still rested on the floor, as if the artist were due back at any moment.

But perhaps most surprising was the fact that the room was filled with hundreds of paintings, some framed but most still unframed canvases. The walls were covered with paintings of the sea, of the harbor, of islanders and tourists and animals. They were all done in the same mystical style.

"He was prolific, I see," said Ryan.

"He didn't sell too much, it's plain to see. No one on the island wanted a picture of something they saw every day. But he was dear to us, was Old Pat Michael. Well, take your time in lookin'."

The man clunked back out to the shop.

Ryan gazed at the paintings that were hung on the walls, only an inch or two between one canvas and another. Even the paintings of desolate rocks exuded a passionate love of the island itself. As he walked slowly about the room, taking them all in, Ryan experienced a vague feeling of unworthiness, as if he didn't understand the subject matter.

He pulled back a couple of paintings in a corner stack, and suddenly stopped. Painted on one of the dusty canvases was a portrait of a nun, and the nun looked like Cleona Owen, her wrinkled face wrapped in white with a black veil atop her head. He pulled the painting from the stack and stared at it in the sunlight. Her face had been painted in a bit of a shadow, but he still thought that it looked like Cleona. He made out a red door behind her head, a couple of chickens in the background. The bottom of the painting had been signed "Pat Michael Dunleavey, 1951."

He brought the painting out to the old man, again seated in the rocking chair.

"Do you know who this is?" he asked the old man.

The man peered closely at the face of the nun and then he shrugged. "Couldn't say for sure. Don't know any nuns, meself."

"I think that it looks exactly like Cleona Owen, in the West Village," said Ryan. "But it was painted in 1951, it says here. And the woman in this painting already appears very...old."

The man nodded. "Pat Michael must have been around 20 years old, when he painted that one. He lived a good part of his life in the West Village, you know," he said, squinting at the face again. "Could be anyone, couldn't it?"

For one nauseous moment, Ryan questioned his own mind. He forced himself to look again at the painting, to perhaps see it in a different light. "This was painted 60 years ago, so the woman in the painting must have already died. Maybe it was of one of Cleona's relatives?"

The man cackled grandly. "Never heard of a nun who was an Owen."

"Does the artist have family here? Someone I could talk to about this painting?"

"No, his daughter is livin' in Dublin now. But she'd be happy to take your money for some of those pictures, so she would."

He'd never purchased art before, but Ryan gave the man some euros for the painting and took it back with him to the hotel. He propped it on the dresser, near the mirror, and the nun's face gazed morosely out at him, already missing the sunlit studio.

∞

He brushed his teeth for the second time that morning and ran his travel brush through his tangled hair, diligent not to catch a glimpse of his swollen face in the mirror. He met Wally in the parlor and together they trundled up and down the hills of the high road toward the West Village.

Wally's cheeks quickly bloomed scarlet as they followed the rambling stone fences up and down the hills, and both of their faces shone with sweat in the unnatural heat of the first day of November. As they neared the West Village, where the hilly fields flattened out in all directions toward the cliffs, they passed by an abandoned cottage. Wally strolled right up to it through the tall grass. He beckoned Ryan closer, the underarms of his plaid shirt darkly wet.

"Come on in," he called. There was nothing to "come in" to,

however. Towering weeds grew in the sandy dirt of the once-square interior.

"Judging from the deterioration, this house was likely abandoned sometime in the early twentieth century," said Wally. "The island can't support a large population, so the young people continue to leave to make their livings."

"The island seems to be doing okay to me," said Ryan. "This village has seen better days, but the East Village is profitable enough."

"This island is fortunate to have such natural beauty and a good harbor, for tourism supports this island now. If it weren't for tourists, this island would go the way of so many others. Abandonment and subsequent purchase by the Irish government as a national park. I've visited an abandoned island not too far from here, and it's a sad, haunted place—all of the cottages look like this one—but still so full of spirit. Great for poets."

"So what will happen to this island, do you think?" asked Ryan. Imagining Aisling and Catherine packing up their few belongings and moving off the island was like imagining fictional characters jumping off the page and eating your dinner.

Wally shrugged. "You never know. The families are broken up and scattered across the globe, and the old ones are all that's left, really. When they pass on, and there's nothing for the younger families to come back to, well...it's hard to say."

Ryan paced the length of the cottage, noting that it seemed about the same size as Aisling's. Wally sat on what was left of an outer stone wall, staring about him at the rocks that once made a home, while the gulls soared low above his head. Ryan reluctantly joined him, disheartened.

Ryan hardly remembered his younger brother Daniel, but he

remembered how uninhabited the house had felt when he and his mother had come home from the double funeral. Overnight, it had become a stranger's house. His mother took to sleeping on the sofa, and the door to Daniel's bedroom had remained closed for three years.

When he was nine years old, Ryan had finally mustered up the courage to peek inside the room. Feeling brave, he removed the safety bar from the bed and forced himself to sit down on the Sesame Street comforter. Then, with a piece of old coloring book and one of Daniel's crayons, he had catalogued all of the items in the room, down to a plastic wheel under the bed and a deflated balloon behind the door. It was a satisfyingly long list.

Perhaps it was the beginning of his interest in archaeology, but Ryan always thought that he was making a list of things death couldn't take. He liked to think that the world could come to an end, but there would always be pen tops somewhere, and broken crayons, items that indicated life.

It had made him feel better, the same way that studying centenarian's DNA samples made him feel superior to death. He beckoned a now-scribbling Wally to follow him as he set off down the road.

∞

At Aisling's cottage, about a dozen local men in baggy suits had gathered inside the gate. Mostly elderly, they smoked pipes and held glasses of whiskey. They stared at Ryan and Wally when they walked through the gate.

"I'll stay out here for now," murmured Wally. "I'm going to

practice my Gaelic on these unsuspecting men. Bring me a plate of food, will you?"

Ryan continued through the doorway. A group of elderly women and a few middle-aged ones stood chatting about the table with plates of food. Some were in the kitchen area, washing dishes in Aisling's bucket and filling glasses with liquor, and the chairs by the hearth were now occupied by elderly women, murmuring to each other. They all wore dark dresses, and their presence rendered the cottage unrecognizable to Ryan.

Dorothy O'Sullivan, appearing youthful in a sea of old, scampered up to him. A big, silver cross gleamed in the center of her ample black chest.

"Mr. Abernathy, they're not entertainin' guests right now!" she whispered, a plump hand sitting heavily on his forearm. "Your business will to have to wait."

"I came to pay my respects."

"Oh, give over. Never heard of Yank comin' to an island wake before," she said. She took in his battered face and broken glasses and tsk-tsked. "My, my. Already found trouble, I see."

"It found me." His entire face throbbed from the mere effort of talking.

"Some folks don't care for tourists here," she said matter-of-factly. She looked about her at the humble cottage. "She was as old as a rock."

She leaned forward and whispered, "Of course Aisling's buryin' her tomorrow in that old pagan cemetery out here. All of their family is buried there, so they are. I wouldn't be goin' there a-tall, if it wasn't for the nun."

"The nun?" asked Ryan curiously, thinking of the nun in the painting.

"Sick with the cancer, so she is," she said sadly. "Always lookin' dead knackered, but wants to come to the funeral."

She puffed out her chest. "I've been helpin' her, so."

"Oh," he said. Ryan peered through the crowd of people. "Have you seen her?"

"The nun?" she asked wildly.

"No, Aisling."

"Sittin' with Cleona now, isn't she?" she answered testily. "It's our custom, so it is."

Embarrassed, Ryan turned to pick up a china plate. He surveyed the table's contents, but was unsure what diet pitfalls were lurking in the dishes. He tried to move closer to what looked like some kind of vegetable dish, but Dorothy put a hand on his shoulder.

"Let's talk of America," she demanded, pulling an elderly woman with a plate of food into her fold. "I'm dying to know more about those wee thingamajigs that play music in your ears. Pods, or puds, is it? They cost a pretty penny, so they do."

"Aye, America is the one with all the devices," agreed the woman, food spewing into the air with the last syllable.

"Oh, aye," agreed Dorothy. "Tell me, Mr. Abernathy. Do you have one of those flat televisions, no wider than a kitchen griddle? Me daughter has three huge ones stuck up on her walls like art. She's even got one in her minivan! The life you Yanks live!"

Ryan put his empty plate down on the table. "Excuse me please. I'm going to pay my respects now."

He stepped away from their wide eyes through the crowded cottage to the lower room. He was relieved to see Aisling, sitting in a chair next to the bed. But he was leery of Cleona's body, stretched out lengthwise on the narrow bed and dressed in a strange costume consisting of a red vest and long, puffy skirt. The window was open, and sunlight illuminated Aisling's pale face, her green, bloodshot eyes.

"You came," she whispered. She wore a black dress that hung shapelessly down to her knees, mud-splattered pantyhose, and cheap black shoes with no heel.

She examined Ryan's bruised face with stricken eyes. "Was it Murray?"

Ryan shrugged, then smiled for her, causing his lip to wail in pain. It didn't matter, he thought. He recalled the morning of his mother's funeral, how unreal the process of getting dressed in his church clothes had been, how silly the act of pouring orange juice into a glass had seemed. He'd held up well to the outside world, but inside him, D-Day took place. He of all people knew how death could flip a person inside out, so that the workings of the heart, the lungs, the guts, were exposed for all to see.

And yet, he couldn't help himself. He stole a glance at Cleona, her skull covered with the merest filigree of skin so that the bones beneath threatened to rupture it. A silver crucifix lay on her chest, and rosary beads were strung through her folded hands.

His eyes lingered on her magnificent white hair. He would only need one strand for a decent DNA sample. If he was left alone with the body, perhaps he could even obtain a cheek swab. A little brush hid inside his back pants pocket. His breath quickened.

He felt Aisling staring at him.

"Where is Catherine?" he asked abruptly. "I thought that she'd be here."

"She can't even raise her head from the pillow. I doubt she'll even be able to come to the funeral tomorrow."

It was all he could do to keep his legs from jiggling atop his toes. "Are you Catholic?" he asked. Usually he never asked people about religious preferences, because it forced him to admit to his own lack of them.

"No," answered Aisling. "Cleona took to the old ways."

"The rosary beads…" he said. "The crucifix on her chest."

"They're Catherine's."

Ryan forced the soles of his shoes into the earthen floor. He nodded sensibly, and wiped his brow with the back of his hand.

"I've been to the church in the East Village several times, with my friend Kiley," Aisling offered. "I liked the Bible stories very much, but once I heard them all, I didn't feel the need to go to church each and every Sunday."

She sat there so rigidly, so composed. He knew this behavior; it was ingrained in him. He remembered the grief as he would a childhood friend he'd purposely distanced himself from, and his heart ached for Aisling. He should say something to her, to let her know he understood.

But his eyes flit to Cleona again. He imagined her genes, still pulsing with life inside her. They beckoned him closer, teased him, but he could do nothing except blink. From the next room, a fiddle's tune broke through the haze, a sad and slow melody that brought silence from the crowd.

An old woman wrapped in a thick shawl entered the room. "Payin' my respects," she murmured. She knelt down by the bed and bowed her head, murmuring a prayer.

When she was done, Ryan helped her to her feet, and she

turned to Aisling. "I'm sorry for your loss, so. She was a good woman."

"Thank you for coming, Mrs. McKiernan," said Aisling.

As she left, another woman came in, and then a man, and then another woman, until the scarlet of the sunset made its way through the window, lighting up the room with red and gold.

Finally, when the stream of mourners ceased, Ryan stood up. "I thought I'd say a little prayer too," he said.

Aisling nodded, her eyes curious. Ryan lowered himself to his knees beside the bed. His back was to Aisling, but even so, he closed his eyes and placed his hands together in prayer. After a few moments, he ran his fingers over Cleona's long hair and yanked at a strand. But the hair was so glossy that his sweaty fingers lost their grip.

Aisling sighed sadly behind him. With shaking hands, he pulled another strand. But in his desperation, he pulled too hard, and Cleona's head fell from the pillow onto the mattress with a thump.

"Whoops," he mumbled. He half-stood and gently pushed her head back onto the pillow. As he did so, he managed to yank a strand from near the back of her shriveled ear.

He stood up again, his heart pounding. He mumbled his regrets to Aisling, and stuffed the long hair into his pants pocket as he stepped quietly from the room.

∞

The cottage was now dark and silent. Only a handful of the oldest islanders remained, their gaunt faces lit by oil lamps. A man with no teeth was telling a story, but Ryan couldn't understand him, for he was speaking in Gaelic.

Ryan spotted Wally on the floor near the door, scribbling like mad in his notebook.

When the old man was finished, an elderly woman took over, again speaking in Gaelic. Heads nodded along, wrinkled lips smiled in remembrance. An old melodeon player took up a tune, and the elderly seemed to absorb the music into their bent bodies. More stories were told, and some brought laughter, some brought tears.

Ryan stood against a white-washed wall, a complete stranger. He gazed from face to pruny face, wondering how he could get DNA samples from all of them. He was willing to bet that their DNA held great secrets—secrets for fighting age and staving off death. He tried not to grin.

After a few more stories, the women made their way into the kitchen, and the men left the cottage, pipes and glasses of liquor in hand.

Ryan found Donal in the group of hunched men, but the man didn't even crack a smile for him. He did manage to survey the injuries to Ryan's face though, and Ryan thought he glimpsed a bit of sympathy in Donal's eyes.

"What were the stories about?" Ryan asked.

"The old days."

"Were they about Cleona?"

"Aye. Some of them were." He took a puff of the pipe, and the smoke wound about this head.

"I don't have any money," teased Ryan.

But Donal wasn't in the mood for jokes. "I don't want your money."

"I want to hear what the stories were about," he said softly, so the other men couldn't hear.

"They don't make a lick of sense in English."

Then he turned to speak with another man about digging the grave tonight. Ryan gathered from the conversation that Murray hadn't been able to attend the wake because he'd been building a casket for Cleona, and now waited in the cemetery with a supply of drink and pipes for all who helped shovel. Ryan felt the shame of the strand of hair, burning his thigh through his pants pocket.

As the men left for the graveyard, Ryan spotted Wally coming out the door of the cottage. Without a word, they began to walk back down the road toward the East Village.

But they hadn't walked ten paces when Ryan stopped. They stood in front of Catherine's darkened cottage, the wisp of chimney smoke that merged into the star-filled sky the only proof that the cottage was inhabited.

"This is her twin sister's home," said Ryan. "She couldn't even come to the wake, right next door."

Wally nodded. "She's gravely ill, they say."

Ryan turned to him in the darkness. "You said that you speak Gaelic."

"That's true," he said. "In fact, the men complimented me on my fluency. I think that's why they let me inside the house. That, and the fact that I'm a writer. The Irish love writers."

"Could you tell me what the stories were about? The ones being told in the cottage?"

He sighed. "Are you familiar with Irish folklore?"

"Not really."

"I wouldn't think you would be," chuckled Wally. "Well, the stories about Cleona and her sister Catherine are truly fascinating, some of the best examples of Irish folklore I've ever heard. My colleagues in the folklore department are going to be very interested in them."

"They're just stories, though," said Ryan. "Fiction?"

Wally smiled mischievously. "You know what they say about stories."

"Behind every story is a grain of truth?" said Ryan skeptically. "Alright, let's hear one."

"One dark and stormy night," he began, snickering. "There once was a witch—Cleona, I believe—who used her dealings with the devil to outwit death, and it was said that she'd been alive for over 200 years. But the witch was lonely after so much life, and used the devil's powers to conjure a likeness of herself. The likeness, who I'm guessing is her twin sister next door, was a source of power for Cleona. She had power over the weather and the seasons, the wind and the rain, the birds and the fish. The devil grew unhappy with her new strong powers, however, and she foretold her death at Samhain—she caused the air to grow strangely warm and the sea to stop—her ancestors came for her soul and took it away. Now the likeness is dying as well, and the devil is looking for a new witch—who happens to be a great-granddaughter of Cleona. The end."

Ryan laughed loudly. "These people can't be that superstitious."

"Perhaps not the younger ones," Wally conceded. "But the old ones still cling to the old ways and beliefs. You'd be surprised what some still believe."

Ryan just shook his head, happy to be a fact-driven scientist.

"Another portrays the twins to be shape-shifters, old women by day and sea gulls by night. According to the story, the women never died, because their souls were being held captive by the devil. They flew about at night, restlessly searching and crying for their souls to be given back. But the devil always refused them, for their souls were pure white, and reminded him of the heaven he'd scorned. The women were said to have been alive on this island for hundreds of years."

The cry of a nearby seagull startled them then, and they laughed.

Wally went on. "They said that the devil grew enchanted by the old women's storytelling, the best he'd heard in the whole world. The gulls finally stole the souls away when the devil was distracted. Some of the locals insisted that they saw two bright lights in the dark sky not too long ago, the lost souls of the old women merging with the birds."

"And then the old women grew sick and died."

"You're catching on brilliantly for a geneticist," said Wally. "I'm sure you noticed the theme of longevity in the stories as well."

"I did," said Ryan. "Hundreds of years old, huh?"

"Give or take a couple of decades," said Wally.

They continued walking down the road in silence, as the ghosts of the abandoned cottages loomed in the moonlight.

"The stories reminded me of something I've read before, but I can't think of the book, or even the context," Wally said. "Have you read any books about the western islands of Ireland?"

"Just a travel guide."

Wally snorted. "I'm not the first writer to have visited this island. Many have come here, looking for inspiration for a novel or a play. And many locals wrote books about nineteenth and early twentieth century life on the western islands. You might be interested in reading some of their work."

"Why?" Ryan hadn't read anything but textbooks in a very long time.

"Like I told you yesterday, the books describe a hard way of life that doesn't really exist anymore. Death was always around the bend. Now, people are so removed from that sensation, so surrounded with comforts and constant stimulation. Life isn't as hard-won, maybe a bit taken for granted."

Speak for yourself, thought Ryan. "That doesn't really have anything to do with *my* work though," he said.

Wally shrugged. "Just thought I'd mention it."

∞

The following day warmed quickly, with a breeze blowing from the southwest.

In contrast, the church seemed uncommonly dark and damp, as Ryan stepped through the door, all sunlight a distant dream. In the pews, he saw the same elderly islanders that had attended the wake. Murray and a few other young men sat near the front.

Ryan tensed; he hadn't been inside a church in a long time.

He slipped quietly into the back pew, but he hadn't escaped the notice of Murray. He turned around and stared at Ryan. Then he said something to the man next to him, who turned and glared at Ryan too.

After a few moments, he caught sight of Aisling walking slowly up the center aisle to the front pew. Aisling smiled briefly at Ryan, who, in the back pew, saw every white and bald head turn toward her. She sat next to Murray, who patted her twice on the shoulder.

The priest emerged from a side door in the front, and soon, it was a maelstrom of incense, prayers and bells, of standing and sitting. Ryan gazed out the windows at the rippling water until the priest mentioned Cleona by name.

"She was well over 100 years old, as you know, and it kept her from coming to mass. But God had a hand in her life, *no matter what some say*. Aye, Cleona Owen was one of the island's special treasures, a visitor from another time altogether."

Only a dozen islanders chose to trek to the West Village for the funeral. The elderly procession ambled slowly, the imported priest at the front, followed by a few men first and some straggling women at the rear. As they walked, Ryan was surprised to see that the blue sky had been replaced with gray clouds. The temperature had dropped a few degrees, but the air was filled with humidity. A couple of old men beside him murmured in wise voices about a coming storm. Ryan pictured his packable rain jacket, back in his suitcase, and hoped the storm would hold off until after the funeral.

When the procession reached the West Village, a few men broke off from the group and entered Cleona's cottage, and Aisling and Murray went inside Catherine's cottage. The men— the younger-looking of the elderly—came out the door a few minutes later bearing the wooden coffin on their shoulders.

When Aisling and Murray emerged in the doorway of Catherine's cottage, they pushed an ancient woman in a rickety wheelchair. Her pale and pruny face peered from beneath a black shawl, knotted tightly beneath her chin, and a wool blanket draped across her lap.

She looked exactly like Cleona, but thinner, more bent; she also looked like the woman in the painting that had stared at him this morning as he'd dressed. Ryan's blood heated at the sight of her. *He would have to get a sample from Catherine soon*, he thought.

Murray carried Catherine and the wheelchair across the threshold and through the gate, out to the road. At the cemetery, the coffin was carefully lowered into the hole the men had dug last night. As the elderly gathered around, Aisling pushed Catherine through the long grass beside the grave. Ryan eyed the place where he'd dug up the grave the night before; he figured it was too far down the overgrown meadow to be noticed.

An elderly nun stood with Dorothy O'Sullivan, and Ryan was almost positive that she had been the one who had checked on him after the ambush. He had an urge to speak to her, but a terrible keening erupted, a high-pitched whine that assaulted his ears.

He looked to find its source, and saw that it was Aisling, her mouth a circle of mourning. She stood, body swaying, beside the open grave, but her gaze was directed at the sky, her palms reaching outward. As the clouds darkened above them, her cry continued for long minutes, until Catherine took it up with the rasping chords of someone much older. Several elderly island women rocked with the same rhythm, and occasionally cried out, startling him.

The gulls made tight circles overhead, pure white against the screen of gray above. The keening grew louder and louder. The entire crowd seemed to move toward one another, united against death.

As he stared at the hole with the coffin inside it, Ryan

remembered how he had watched his mother die, soon after she'd repeatedly muttered "eagles" in a morphine-induced trance. Death had come quickly in the end, and he had stood there next to it, more alive than he'd ever felt in his short life.

He liked to think that she had flown into a golden, glittering light, but deep down he knew that it had only been that black, anonymous death that had taken the life from her. She had flown nowhere, had descended into invisibility; the birds had deceived her.

The cold, black cemetery soil was a perfect ending place for such a disaster. He'd watched her coffin descend into the ground, and vowed that he'd never find himself in such a forgotten place.

Get on with it, he urged the priest.

The two women wailed, until the priest, in silken, white robes that whipped in the strong wind, finally began to give the short graveside service. When it was over, and the two women were silent, dirt was flung into the hole, and winkle shells were thrown atop the grave. There was no stone marker yet, no carved dates of life.

Aisling and Murray wheeled a slumping Catherine back down the road, and the funeral-goers parted. There was talk of the pub amongst the old men.

The graveyard was too quiet then, and Ryan made his way back down the road. Yet he'd soon caught up with the elderly islanders, so he chose to cut across a field to find the less traveled low road. He walked a while on the road, but then felt unsure of his destination. He had the overwhelming sense that what he wanted, and needed, was back the way he'd come.

He veered off the road and soon found the white sand of the beaches. He sat down on the sand and faced the angry ocean, its recent slumber disturbed. He felt an icy rain drop land on his nose and crawl down the slope to the tip, where it evaporated into the wind.

He thought of Aisling, now the lone occupant of the cottage. Would Murray be there, trying in his gruff manner to comfort her? He saw Aisling as she appeared during the keen; her back had been held regally straight, her cheeks, still pale, had bloomed two rosy circles in their centers. Her hair had blown crazily about her head. She had appeared utterly alone, the only woman on earth. He had thought her beautiful then, but he'd kicked himself for thinking such thoughts while her great-grandmother rested in the ground beneath her feet.

Yet graveyards, he knew, had a way of focusing one's attention on things that mattered most. The stones themselves were a warning to the living. *Your time will come,* they whispered.

Ryan had taken the warning seriously.

As he continued to sit, the wedge of dark clouds closed in on him. The wind thumped his body, and the drops picked up speed and frequency, gathering for a feast. He decided to head back to Aisling's cottage. There was more that he wanted to say to her.

∞

He knocked on the blue door and very soon it opened. Aisling faced him, and the cottage loomed darkly behind her. She let out a long, steady sigh, as if she'd been holding her breath.

"I...I just wanted to see how you were doing," he said. He peered past her into the black. "Is Murray here?"

"No," she said. "Couldn't wait to get to the pub."

He nodded, trying not to show his relief. "Well, I didn't like the idea of you all alone in here."

As Ryan stood there on Aisling's threshold, his shirt grew damp with rain. But she seemed not to notice.

"Can I come in for a few moments?" he asked. "Until the rain stops?"

She opened the door a bit wider, and Ryan walked inside. He heard her close the door. Then she walked past him and seated herself in a chair by the hearth. She motioned to the opposite chair. He sat down, and she picked up a gray ball of yarn and squeezed it between her fingers.

He wanted to hug her to him. "Are you alright?"

She nodded. "She lived a long life."

"Yes. That's a comfort."

They sat in silence for a long time, as the sky beyond the rain-wet windows dimmed to a slate gray.

"I would give anything," he finally said. "To live a long life."

She raised curious eyes to his. "You like life so very much?"

"No..." He shook his head back and forth, fearing the buried emotions that were rising up inside him. He took a deep breath, and the words suddenly escaped from his mouth like vomit.

"I'm afraid to die." The fear, so ingrained in him, felt like a sickness, an embarrassment.

She studied his face for a moment. Then she got up to look out the window through the gasping light at the pitted sea, at its layer of matching clouds.

"No one knows what's on the other side," she said.

"I have a pretty good idea," he said, unable to help himself. "Nothing. Nothing is on the other side. It's terrifying."

Death was anti-life, anonymity. He could hardly think of not existing without breaking into a sweat.

"You can try to imagine death, but it's impossible. It's like trying to see the wind," she said. "I like *not* knowing."

A warm tear leaked from his eye, stinging the wound on his cheekbone. He sighed raggedly, unable to speak. He was useless; he had come here to comfort her, to offer her something—some wise proclamation—that he'd learned from experiencing the death of loved ones, but now *she* was the one comforting *him*.

Perhaps he'd learned nothing valuable at all, he thought sadly.

"I have to know, you see," said Ryan. "I need facts."

She gave him a small smile. "I know."

Again they lapsed into silence. She still stood by the window. *She didn't seem crazy now*, he thought. *She just seemed lonely.*

"Was Cleona really...as old as you said she was?"

"Aye," she said.

He wanted to believe her; the oldest people in the world could have lived here on the island. Aisling made it look possible. Her eyes reflected the island, her face told its history.

He thought that maybe, for once, he didn't require facts to know the truth.

∞

He got up from the chair then and stepped slowly to the window. She watched him carefully as he raised a hand to her cheek. He heard the wood pop in the hearth as his hand hovered in the air.

Then he touched her cheek with his whole hand and could

feel the warmth of the blood pulsing beneath the cold flesh. He rubbed the cheek just a bit. He couldn't stop himself. Under his probing fingers, Aisling's skin was tautly smooth and mocked the age-smudged skin of his hand.

It was life itself that pulsed in her body. What if her muscles, her bones, her nervous system, her mucous membranes—every part of her was filled with the promise of incredible longevity?

He leaned closely to her and inhaled her scent of turf smoke and herbs. And then, he barely brushed his swollen lip to her mouth. He wanted more; he believed that he could hear her genes whispering to him, and he wanted to suck the blood from her lip. He wanted to lick her teeth, mash her tongue, in spite of the pain it would cause him.

Instead, he shook his head to clear it, and breathed in and out, over and over. And just the act of breathing made his head spin with pleasure. He had taken it for granted all of these years.

He looked into her green, unworldly eyes, wanting her with a howling ache in his torso, the opposite of the anxiety that usually clenched it. Now, his breath came out of his mouth like fire.

Aisling hooked his face with both of her hands and smashed her lips against his. At first, his nerves registered pain and he flinched away, but the sensation was soon overridden with the simple pleasure of meeting a woman's lips, something he hadn't done in a very long time.

Her mouth told him of her sadness, a devastating loneliness. But beneath that, he learned of a stubborn passion, much bigger than the island, the rocky ground under his feet.

13

Sister Ignatius had attended many funerals. However, this one on the island was the first she'd attended next to the mighty ocean.

Her black habit fit in well with the somber attire of the islanders. It seemed that only a few, mostly elderly, locals had chosen to attend the funeral; they nodded politely at her and some doffed their caps.

Dorothy O'Sullivan stood protectively next to her. The mourners' faces shifted and heads hung. They murmured to each other, their dirt-encrusted shoes shuffled. The scene made her feel old, defeated—that it was too late for her.

She had wanted to come to the funeral to feel more alive. And yet she saw the clouds, an endless night, closing in on her. She took a deep shuddering breath and tried to remind herself that death was a homecoming, that God was watching over her.

Then, with surprise, she saw the man who had been beaten and pulled to the side of the road the night before. She'd heard his stifled cries through the warm air of her room, and her skin had tingled as if the devil himself were there. And today, his face was almost grotesque.

She realized how easy it would be for Satan to hold sway on this battered rock, far out in the deep sea. It would be so easy for him to find roots among the crumbling stones.

She'd had gone to see to the beaten man, unsure what she meant to do. Once she found him, in the rocks beside the road, she gazed at him for several long minutes. In the moonlight, she saw the broken glasses, several feet from his body, and placed them carefully on his head.

Then she'd touched his cheek. She'd never touched a man before, not even a priest, not even her father. She hardly even touched her fellow sisters. She was surprised how good it felt, this basic act, the warm skin and life beneath her fingers. She had absorbed the God-given gift she'd felt in him, and had left him there, feeling that she had somehow done her duty. Walking away, she'd smelled the sea on her habit, and last night, she'd slept more peacefully than she'd done in months.

Her eyes drifted from the man to the dead woman's elderly sister, seated in a wheelchair off to the side. Sister Ignatius studied the face, a smushed oval peering gloomily from beneath a kerchief, at first just to commit it to her memory so that she could include the woman in her prayers that night.

But the more she stared, the more she remembered, as if she were reading a familiar part of the Bible and was reminded of her first impressions. Her skin grew hot in her habit, as she recalled the prayerful eyes, the humble position of the head on the neck.

She looked away, then back again, peering even more closely. When the old woman's voice broke into the keen, she knew that she'd heard its rough tenor before, ringing through a chapel, singing hyms. Her mind hummed with memories long buried. She hardly felt the wind whip her habit about her body.

When the service was over, and the mourners were making their way back to their homes before the rain came, she told Dorothy that she'd like to linger in the cemetery for a while. With a pinched face and a giant huffing, Dorothy promised to return soon.

Sister Ignatius followed the old woman and the young woman and man helping her, watched them enter a small cottage down the road. After a few moments, the young people left the cottage and entered the cottage next door.

Alone on the road, Sister Ignatius stood before the cottage, a square dwelling of twelve feet, if that. She knocked on the door and waited for several minutes, but she heard neither a voice nor footsteps.

Sister Ignatius couldn't wait. She opened the door and walked cautiously into the gloom. A straw St. Brigid's cross hung crookedly over a narrow bed that rested against the back wall. The old woman barely made a lump in the gray wool blanket.

Without the black kerchief, her hair was mostly gray fuzz, spread like moss over a white scalp. Her ashen, spotted skin hung in intricately pressed creases over her face, down her skinny neck. She was as immobile as a corpse.

Sister Ignatius stepped closer to the bed and peered closely at her face.

"Sister Ambrose?" she barely whispered. She said the name louder, and the woman jerked, her milk-glass eyes wide and wary.

Sister Ambrose had disappeared from the convent over sixty years ago, with no letter, no forwarding address. The convent had been worried, because Sister Ambrose had been 119 years old at the time. Sister Ignatius had known her only a short while, but she had admired her devotion, her God-given gift of healthy old age.

And now, here she was on a remote island. She was still alive.

"Who are you?" Sister Ambrose croaked.

"How are you still alive? It's been over sixty years," Sister Ignatius breathed. "It—it's a miracle!"

Exhalation swayed the gray hairs in Sister Ambrose's nostrils, and the woman's eyes loomed like gateways to nowhere. The wind screamed through the window, not quite shut, and ricocheted off the white-washed walls. Sister Ignatius suppressed a shudder and crouched down on the earthen floor. She took the woman's twisted hands gently in her own, and they trembled inside Sister Ignatius's grasp. She closed her eyes and forced her galloping mind to slow, to think.

It stretched back to her first year in the convent, when her pride had flared from her with undeniable heat. She hadn't wanted to become a nun; nuns answered to priests, bishops, *men with higher rank*. Nuns had no power.

A convent, cloistered from the world, went against her nature. She was accustomed to poverty and chastity, but it had taken her many years to grow used to the subservience. It had taken much longer to rein in her ambition, to match herself to her fellow sisters. A requirement for her convent, she had taken a male saint's name.

Of course she remembered the woman on the bed. It had been Sister Ambrose who had helped Sister Ignatius to find pride in the convent and in her calling. As old as Sister Ambrose was— the convent believed her to be the oldest woman in the world— she still worked alongside Sister Ignatius in the walled garden; she had had the stamina of a much younger woman. They ordered new seeds and bulbs, weeded and watered several times a day, pruned and prayed during the winter; the following spring the garden bloomed as it never had before. Sister Ignatius had grown more content, and Sister Ambrose had continued to live.

The old woman on the bed now craned her neck to peer at Sister Ignatius. She beckoned Sister Ignatius closer, so Sister Ignatius leaned over the withered face, as close as she could get.

"I remember you," the woman whispered.

Sister Ignatius's coif squeezed her forehead too tightly, and she tried not to laugh hysterically. "Aye," she said.

The two women stared at each other.

"I...I have a brain tumor that won't stop its growing. I won't last long," Sister Ignatius blurted.

Then, in a calmer voice, she said, "Why did you leave us, sister? We prayed for you for many years."

Sister Ambrose studied the loose, mottled skin of her hands. She didn't respond for a long moment, and when she looked up at Sister Ignatius, her eyes seemed not to know her anymore.

"Sister Ambrose," she urged. She sat cautiously down on the narrow bed. "I was Evie O'Grady. Remember?"

The woman stared at a spot above Sister Ignatius's head. In the silence, Sister Ignatius heard the rain begin to fall on the road outside. She got up and closed the window, then seated herself on the bed again. Her scalp under the coif itched savagely.

"I was prideful, ambitious," Sister Ignatius continued. "When I was a novitiate, I was made to lay down by the kitchen door so that the sisters would have to walk over me to get their food. Do you remember that? I was told to walk with my hands under the scapula, to keep my eyes down, and too many times I ate meals off the dining room floor."

She paused to take a deep breath. "Do you remember the garden? We scattered the daffodil seeds over that open area between the trees...do you remember how well they bloomed? It was a field of yellow and white that spring, where before it had been dried mud. The daffodils still bloom."

The rain pounded the window, scattered stones on glass. Sister Ambrose closed her eyes. "God bless you, sister," she finally whispered.

"You must be very old. Aye, very old indeed," Sister Ignatius marveled.

She could see how a young woman would have received the calling here, on the island; it must have sounded like an old bell, ringing on the top of a snow-covered mountain in a pure, blue sky. Perhaps it was why she had returned.

She removed the camera from the pocket of her habit and with shaking hands, snapped a photograph of Sister Ambrose's face.

God had chosen Sister Ambrose. And God had chosen Sister Ignatius to find her. Despite the growing storm, there was an aura of gold in the room. As she took Sister Ambrose's hands in hers, she felt the blessings pour into her sickened body.

14

Ryan gazed about the interior of the cottage once again. It was only now that he noticed how utterly barren the cottage was of modernity. There was no television, no radio, no refrigerator, no computerized devices of any kind. He didn't even see any books. He spotted nets and fishing lines in a little loft over the hearth. He figured they had once belonged to Aisling's father, Michael.

The motley platters of bread and cake and stew from the wake still occupied most of the table. Aisling added some turf to the fire and began placing bread and cold boiled potatoes onto chipped china plates. Neither spoke as they ate, and Ryan hadn't known that food could taste as good as it did, sitting across from Aisling at a worn, wooden table.

Aisling put the dishes in a bucket to soak, and then pulled a checkered duvet from her loft in the bedroom to stretch beside the fire. Ryan went to sit next to her, but his hands remained glued to his thighs. He heard the wind blow against the front door.

Undisturbed, Aisling leaned over and nibbled on his earlobe, and he shied away, more because of her brazenness than the sensation.

"You're just like Murray," she teased.

"How do you mean?"

"He never looks at me."

He turned his head, and in the waning hearth light, her head appeared to be on fire. He reached out to touch her jawbone with an unsure hand, half-expecting her to vanish into the chiaroscuro. Her skin was hot now, with a hint of dampness.

She pulled his head down to her lap and wound her fingers through his hair. And her voice fluttered as she told of old, old island people who believed that living a long life was a blessing from the gods, and of the offspring of long-lived elders who mated with other offspring of long-lived elders, before the time of Stonehenge, and long before Jesus.

These people produced more long-lived children who grew to mate with others of their kind. Over the millennia, the islanders grew older and older, outliving other humans by many years. They were strong and healthy, even in old age. The island protected them. And yet, their lines gradually weakened. Babies were harder to conceive, and some mothers, and babies, died in the birthing. Children were cursed with disease. The clan was no longer favored. Others came ashore; Vikings, monks, Normans, and English plundered and exploited. The world outside the island beckoned. The elders grew fewer and fewer, until there remained only a handful left.

"That's quite a story," said Ryan, his head still resting on her thighs.

"Cleona told it to me when I was barely able to follow along. I remember feelin' very special after that."

Ryan nodded. He told himself that it was just a story. "Some words we hear as children never let us go."

Aisling touched his neck, the skin under his collar, with warm fingers.

His tongue loosened in the warming light of the fire. "My dad and younger brother Daniel died in a car accident when I was six. My mother died of cancer when I was eleven, and then her parents died too. I don't have any other relatives. No cousins, no long-lost aunts or uncles. I'm the last in the line too."

She pushed him down on the duvet and straddled him, her hands placed firmly on his shoulders.

"Americans...we've lost a sense of our ancestry. I never knew mine; it wasn't important to my parents, I guess. But now, it's like my whole history is blank."

Her hair hung down, smelling of rosemary. He tried to concentrate. *Was this really what he was aching to tell her?* He'd never told anyone any of this before.

Aisling licked his swollen lip, his bruised bones. His breath quickened, and he strained to speak. "For my mom, I tried as hard as I could to live. I didn't ride my bike in traffic. I didn't go outside in storms. I didn't enter large bodies of water. I washed my hands at least 50 times a day."

She unzipped his pants, an alien sound amid the popping fire. She pulled her black dress over her head, and he saw that she wore no bra, only a worn pair of white, cotton underwear under her nude stockings. She removed them slowly, the hairs along her legs upright in the flames.

"I want to live a long time. That's why I study as hard as I do. I want to understand...longevity...help people."

He trailed off, couldn't think anymore. Her thighs gripped his hips, her strong hands rubbed his chest. He smelled her musky odor.

As she moved on top of him, he didn't think of DNA or genetics, of health and longevity and capsules and vitamins. His only thoughts, if he had them at all, swirled out the hole in the roof and blew with the smoke into the rain-filled air.

∞

Ryan smelled the rain in his dreams filled with oceans and cliffsides, and he half-remembered reaching for Aisling's naked body during the night, never knowing which part of her was touching.

Sometime in the morning, he was brutally awakened by a thumping outside Aisling's cottage. He then heard a knock on the door, loud and insistent and meant to awaken. Aisling stirred at his side, unwrapping her arms and legs from his body. Looking at Ryan with anxious eyes, she put a finger to her lips.

"Aisling!" came Murray's voice. "Wake on up, girl."

Grey daylight made its way through the cracks in the wood of the door. The rain still splattered heartily on the roof overhead.

"I'm awake, Murray. You can stop your shoutin'."

"Well come on out and see me then. Your face is a damned sight better than this door."

Ryan heard him try to push the door open, but the latch held firmly.

Aisling squeezed her eyes shut. "Thank you for the compliment, but I think I heard your mam calling you."

"You're a clever one for a girl who just lost her granny. I brought you somethin'."

"I hope it's not a rottin' hunk of seal meat."

"I wouldn't be wastin' it on the likes of you, would I? Come on, girl, I'm gettin' drowned."

"I'm not feelin' well, Murray. Women's business. Come back later."

He was silent for a few moments. "There's some turf from my own stack, here on your front step. Don't worry about thankin' me, now."

"I won't."

"Best bring it in before the rain gets to it," he warned.

They listened to him walk to the window, covered by sagging curtains. His silhouette swam darkly for a while, then it disappeared.

Aisling sighed, her creamy forehead tracked with lines.

He stroked the sharp slope of her jaw. "Would he ever hurt you? Because of me?"

"No, he'd hurt *you*," she said, running a spread of fingers along his swollen cheek. "And I don't think your face can take much more."

"I won't hide from him."

"I know."

Then she kissed him, her nose pressing so hard into his that it blocked the air. He grew dizzy and flopped back on the duvet. He pressed his hands into her back, bringing her body, her blood, even closer to his. And then he felt her heartbeat through her breasts, through his sternum.

"Your quest for long life reminds me of a popular Irish tale," said Aisling. "About Oisin and Niav?"

"I'm not much when it comes to stories," he said. "You know that."

"Oisin—a strong and brave warrior—is taken by Niav of the Golden Hair, the daughter of the god of the sea who reigns over *Tír na nÓg,* to the World of the Forever Young."

"I do like the sound of that," said Ryan. "Can I get a flight there?"

Aisling put her finger to his lips. "It's a place beyond the edges of the map, on an island far to the west of Ireland. It's a place beyond the senses, where sickness and death don't exist, a place of eternal youth, strength and beauty, where music, poetry, and community come together. Food and drink aren't needed, and happiness lasts forever."

"Is *Tír na nÓg* like heaven? Where people go when they die?"

"No, it's part of the Otherworld, a mystical place that exists alongside our world, just out of sight," she said. "Full of gods and goddesses, fairies and spirits. Mortals can go there, but they can't stay."

Ryan licked her palm and tasted salt, perhaps thyme. He wound his hand through her long hair.

"Oisin goes there to be with Niav and spends his life writing poetry and songs, but he eventually becomes homesick and wants to visit his own world once more. Niav warns against this, but Oisin is stubborn and sets out on Niav's magical white horse, in order to obey Niav's warning not to set foot on Irish soil. When he returns, Oisin realizes that 300 years have passed while he was living in *Tír na nÓg,* and saddened, decides to return to

Niav. But on the way back, he comes across some men tryin' to lift a heavy rock and bends down to help them. But he slips from the saddle and falls to the ground, where he instantly begins to age—his hair becomes brittle and gray, his skin thin and wrinkled, his strength gone."

"Now that's a tragedy," he said. "I guess the moral of the story is 'don't fall off your horse.'"

"Is that all you took from the tale?" she asked, running a finger down the center of his chest.

He took his hand from her hair and sighed. "No, I guess not. Maybe the story is trying to say that living an eternally perfect life in an exotic locale isn't all it's..." he exhaled loudly. "Who are we kidding? Isn't that what everyone wants, when it comes down to it? To live a rich, comfortable life with the one you love? To never have it end in death and old age?"

"Such a life doesn't satisfy the soul of a person."

"It sounds good enough to me."

"A life well-lived needs hard work, sacrifice, the joy of watchin' things grow," she said. "None of that can happen in *Tír na nÓg*, where only pleasure and joy exist."

He still disagreed. "'A great place to visit, but you wouldn't want to live there.' I see how it is." His fingers found her hair again. "Do you...believe in this Otherworld place?"

"Of course," she said. "What you *see* isn't all there is, Ryan."

He knew she would respond that way. He began to suspect that the woman lived her entire life within these stories. And yet, he too felt the pull of the stories, so that his future—a United States laboratory, a genetics dissertation—seemed vaguely ridiculous.

∞

They hadn't ventured from the cottage all day. Ryan had listened, hour after hour, as Cleona's stories became Aisling's. He hadn't even known that people like Aisling existed. He thought he would have become bored with the stories after a while, but he'd found himself lost in forests, on mountain tops, on the decks of ships, and he'd lost all track of time.

She'd told of gods and goddesses, of heroes and heroines, of fairies and selkies and leprechauns. Her face and voice had transformed, her arms had risen and flown around her as she spun her tales. She'd spoken in both Gaelic and English, sometimes unaware of the switch.

Aisling now lay next to him in the shape of a question mark, her breasts touching his back, her knees stuck in the crook of his legs. The fire burned low, dark red, and the stories had stopped.

"Do you ever get sick? What do you eat?" he asked.

"I don't get sick very much," she murmured into his neck. "And I eat when I'm hungry. It isn't often."

He believed her. They hadn't eaten a thing that day except leftover cake.

She kissed his back so lightly that he thought perhaps he was imagining it. "And Cleona and Catherine...was it the same with them?"

"Aye, but Catherine lived most of her life on the mainland."

He rolled over and faced her, as the sweat cooled on his back. "Really?"

"She came back to the island when she got too old."

"Too old for what?" Ryan's head spun. "Did she have children? A husband? Where did she live? What did she do?"

He thought of Donal's story about Catherine's sudden appearance on the island. She did have another life somewhere, and he suddenly longed to know what it was.

"I don't know. Catherine never told me, as far as I can remember. Her mind was all but gone when I was born. She prayed a lot."

"What about Cleona?" he urged. "In all of her stories, Cleona never told you anything about her *twin sister*?"

"No," she said sadly. "Just stories about when they were children. They didn't get along. And then Catherine left the island for a long time. Cleona had to care for her mother and father, her grandparents too."

Ryan thought of Catherine's rosary beads, the crucifix. "Do the islanders know anything about Catherine?"

"No one has lived long enough to know," she said simply. "They can only guess."

Finally, he felt a stab of frustration at her naivety. She ran a finger over his knotted eyebrows.

"You'd have to live here to understand," she said. "Truth is covered in myth. It isn't as important here."

He groaned. He had the urge to put his glasses back on, to see things more clearly.

She traced the outline of his swollen lip. "The islanders believe what they want to believe. Isn't it the same with you?"

"I guess I'm more of a scientist," he admitted.

There had been unhappy and desperate times in his life when he'd wished he could transcend the realities of his life, dive into another realm of faith or movie-magic. But something in him had clung to the order, the scientific facts, of life. It made more sense to him; it comforted him, in the face of his losses.

∞

Early the next morning, Ryan woke with the realization that not only had he missed the ferry back to the mainland, but he'd also missed his flight back to the U.S.

He thought for a moment of Theo and his professors, waiting on him Monday morning, guessing that, for once, Ryan Abernathy must have been too sick to attend classes.

Ryan's chest squeezed a bit, thinking of those that he'd shunned for his own selfish needs. He'd sent a couple of cryptic text messages—and a slightly longer one to Rose.

But when he attempted to use the chemical toilet in the bedroom, he chuckled to himself, all thoughts of America gone. The contraption was like a toilet training potty for adults, and he had a hard time imagining Aisling using it, and cleaning it, day after day.

He stood and stretched his arms over his head, relishing the way his muscles sang in release. He looked on the humble surroundings with affection. He thought of the journal that Dr. Buxton had given him, and found himself wishing he'd brought it along.

The rain had stopped sometime in the night, but the wind still prowled around the cottage. Wan daylight snuck around the cracks in the curtains. Aisling still slept on the duvet, her red hair winding like vines from beneath a blanket. He imagined her dreams to be full of color and sound and peopled with the characters in her stories.

He crept out the door of the cottage with the water buckets and made his way to the stream, whistling the tune to the song that Aisling had sung to him the day before. The foggy island seemed alive with spirits now; he expected to catch glimpses of the Good People, lurking behind wet rocks and tombstones, watching him. He looked to the rumbling ocean, half-searching for the horses and cattle that were said to live in the water, for the Otherworld ships that appeared out of nowhere, bringing either luck or disaster to the sailors.

Mist hung over the gray stream, and he grinned as he imagined coming across a mermaid on one of the rocks. If she saw him before he saw her, she would curse him and take him with her, down to the Otherworld. He would have to be careful.

He scooped the water gently into the buckets and made his way back up the hill, his arms protesting with the weight, and the feeling of his back being pushed was like unexpected thunder. He stumbled, spilling the water in all directions.

He turned to see Murray, his face unrecognizable in his anger. Ryan expected to feel frightened, yet he stood his ground. He watched Murray struggle for words, his mouth curling over several possible contenders.

"I gave you fair warning," he finally spat.

"Aisling won't like it if you hurt me again."

He cringed at how childish the words sounded. But his face still pained him terribly from the beating Murray had given him, and he wasn't anxious to extend the damage to other body parts.

"Aisling doesn't know what you're about," Murray rasped, his arms shivering with want of use. "But I do. And I've kept her and her family from ill-wishers like you for years now."

"So you're *protecting* her?"

"Aye," he said. "You've got it now."

"They have a name for men like you in America," he said. "Stalkers. They go to jail."

"Call it what you will, so," shrugged Murray. He tried to smile. "When your face patches up, you won't be too bad to look on. Don't you have some four-eyes woman waitin' on you back home?"

"No."

"Millions of women in the world, and you want Aisling."

"Yes. She's special."

"*I've* known her since she was a girleen. I think I know her a wee bit better than you."

His black eyes burned again, but his voice lacked its original bite.

He suddenly collapsed onto his backside, as if he'd been working for days without rest or food. Ryan stood quietly beside him, careful not to make any large movements. They were silent for several minutes, as the sky slowly lightened around them.

"I guess you and her..." Murray couldn't continue.

"Yes," said Ryan. He braced himself for bodily contact.

Murray just nodded. "She's tellin' you all manner of stories, so that you can't even think a single thought in your own head?"

"A little." Ryan was glad that Murray had chosen not to rough him up again, but he wasn't willing to share such intimate details with him.

"That's what she does," said Murray. He shook his head violently, tiny drops of moisture falling about his face. "I can't abide it. I wish she'd just act like a normal *woman*."

Ryan cleared his throat, but didn't say anything.

"Most people don't know what to think of her," he said. "She's pretty enough, aye. But they think she's touched in the head, you know. Tellin' all those stories, you can't hardly know the truth from her. And comin' from that queer family of hers, people don't treat her the way they should."

Murray rubbed his hands over his stubbled face. "I saw it in her eyes that day you first came," he said. "'Twas someone new and different for her."

"Is there something... not right about her?" Ryan asked, suddenly ashamed of himself.

He snorted. "And *you're* askin' *me*?"

Murray spoke through his fingers, his voice lower and rougher. "I'll tell you, just for your own good. Me grandmother used to tell terrible tales about her and her family. Things that she'd seen and heard over the years, livin' right down the road from 'em."

"What kinds of stories?"

Murray shook his head violently, and his voice dropped to a whisper. "Awful things that kept me up at night. Misshapen babies that could only speak the devil's language. Queerly pretty little children that could see their own terrible futures, old women and men that lived for hundreds of years because they'd sold their souls to Satan."

Murray shook his head, back and forth. "Somethin' in me believes what they say about her. There's something in her eyes, her skin, the way she talks, and spins those stories, like she's not even human. Gives me a gut-wrenchin' fear, so it's all I can do not to run away from her."

Ryan had a hard time imagining Murray running away from a beautiful woman.

Murray whispered, "I told her I'd marry her. But I'll tell you, I don't want children with her. What if they turn out half-fairy?"

Ryan stared at Murray. He was nothing more than a child in a grown man's body.

"Don't say I didn't warn you," muttered Murray. He stood up and gazed about him, an almost fearful look in his eyes.

"I need a pint," he finally said.

Then he loped away, his giant shoulders slumped forward. Another island creature, a relic from a lost time.

∞

Ryan returned with two full buckets of water, and still Aisling slept. He undressed and layed down beside her, all thoughts of Murray gone. Her eyelids twitched, and he wondered if she dreamed of Cleona. He also wondered if, in the telling of the stories, Aisling was celebrating Cleona's life, dealing with the loss.

"Why don't you tell *me* one, then?" she murmured from beneath the blanket.

"A story?"

She pulled the blanket from her face and grinned at him, her eyelids still weighty with recent sleep. "Aye, a story. Somethin' about yourself."

He thought for a while, but most of the events in his life were boring, not worthy of a story by the hearth. He could only think of one, and he wasn't sure why he had arrived at the particular story. But it somehow seemed important to him now.

He stared at the whitewashed ceiling, trying to remember. "When my mother died, I was 11 years old, and I flew with her parents to Indiana to live with them on their farm."

"Indiana?"

"It's a state. In America. Farms everywhere you look. It was very different from the city in Virginia where I grew up. My grandparents had several hundred acres."

"Were they very rich?"

"No," he laughed. "They got by though. I sat between them in the front seat of their rusty blue truck on the way to the farm. I remember feeling very sad. My grandparents talked about pigs and chickens, hoping to pique my interest I guess. When we drove down the dusty lane toward the farmhouse, I spotted two horses in the field. They were playing, I thought.

"I said, 'Hey, granddad! That horse is getting a piggyback ride!'"

Aisling moaned. "I believe I know what you saw!" she said. "Go on, then."

"Well, granddad started laughing so loud that I had to cover my ears. Grandma giggled politely behind her hand. And it was good to hear them laughing, I remember, because they were sad too. After catching his breath, granddad said, 'I don't know how Martha May stands it. Lionel is too young for that old girl.' I remember he took one hand off the grimy steering wheel and patted my knee. He said, 'In a couple years, I'll explain how they do it.'

"I figured there wasn't much to explain about a piggyback ride. But when Martha May fell to the ground, and stayed there for twelve hours straight because she couldn't get up, and then died two days later, I knew there was something about piggyback rides that I didn't understand."

Aisling groaned, and buried her head in his armpit.

"For a couple of months, I hated Lionel for hurting Martha May so badly, all for a stupid game of piggyback. But I soon learned the truth, because living on a farm taught me a few things."

"Things?" she teased.

"Well, you know," he hedged. "Things about...having babies and waste elimination and awful stuff that I couldn't watch. It was all so messy. My grandparents took pity on me, I think. For the rest of my teenage years, they sheltered me from farm life. I learned how to clean and polish wood, wash windows, shake out hooked rugs, dust my grandma's porcelain children with the chubby faces."

He paused, as memories flooded his mind. He suddenly wished that he hadn't told this story; he had too much buried regret.

"What became of them?"

"I went away to college and never really came back. I loved my grandparents. But they were getting older, and soon after I left, they sold their farm and checked themselves into a retirement facility nearby."

"You left them there?"

"It's what we do in America," he said. "There are nursing homes and facilities full of elderly everywhere you look. It's a booming industry."

His nose began to drip, and he swiped at it with the back of his hand. "They died within days of each other. I'd been too busy with my exams to even attend the funerals. My only family."

Aisling laid a hand on his bare chest, wiggled her fingers through the light brown hairs. "They are still with you," she said, as if reading his fortune in the squiggles.

Her words brought such peace then, a fresh coating of snow on rough branches of pain. She knew about life and death; she accepted her fate gracefully, with arms out, as if to greet an old friend. He knew now that she wasn't simple or slow at all; she was brighter even than he.

"Tell me about life on the island, the way that it was a long time ago," he said. "I've heard that it was a hard life."

He found, then, that Aisling knew the old island life as well as if she'd lived through it herself. She told of how crews of men oared curraghs, even in the roughest seas, to throw out nets for fish, how a single shark could provide oil for the island's lamps for over a year, how the people ate nothing but potatoes and fish and bread.

He kept his eyes closed, but pulled her body to him as he covered them with a blanket. She told him of relatives long ago passed, their hardships and simple joys. The stories grew on each other, blending and backtracking and then building again, until she was speaking of her own mother.

"Orla—my mam—had finally held a baby to term, after many losses, and she was full of joy. But the baby had sapped the life from her, making her so tired that she couldn't leave the bed for three months. When her time neared, Orla was as white as a gull's feather, as thin as a reed. She had no strength to birth the baby, and she died before the baby was even out of her belly. Cleona'd seen it all before, with her daughter and grand-daughter as well, so with great sadness, she reached inside and pulled the baby out. And one look at the child washed her sadness away, for she held in her arms the power of the clan's blood line. The girl baby radiated life and health as no other had, and Cleona prophesied that the girl would never leave the island. She would be the last of the line," Aisling finished. "She named the girl Aisling, for the vision."

"What does it all mean?" he asked.

"Our line—the island family—has died out. I will be the last."

Suddenly, he wanted to help her, to pull her out of these endless stories for a while, so that she could see something different for herself.

"You could leave the island with me," he said.

She shook her head firmly. Then she said, tentatively, "How?"

She squeezed his hand hard, held it to her navel.

"First, we would take the ferry to the mainland. Then we'd get in the rental car at the harbor and drive to the airport. Then we'd take an airplane across the ocean."

"To America," she said softly.

"You'd love America. Mountains, beaches, deserts, anything you could ever want to see."

He ran his finger across the lines of her palm. He tried to imagine Aisling in the States, shopping at the grocery store and driving a car and going to the gym, but it was like imagining a mermaid walking from the sea on two human legs and trying to speak English but squawking like a gull instead.

When Ryan's cell phone vibrated with a text, they both stirred. After a while, he got up, searching for his boxers. Aisling settled back into the wool blankets, a long pale arm draped across her body.

The text was from Rose.

"How goes the sampling with the sister? Dad wants to know."

He sighed, suddenly frustrated. *What was he doing?* He sat down on the mattress beside Aisling. She reached for his phone still in his hand and ran her long fingers over the buttons. She held it upside down and spoke Gaelic into it. He thought of Catherine, next door this entire time.

"Your ancestors," he began, too loudly.

She twirled strands of his hair on her forefinger, pulling his head toward her.

"The ones in the graveyard where Cleona was buried," he continued. "One of the tombstones indicates an extremely long life."

She looked at him curiously, let go of his hair. "Aye?"

"Well, seeing that grave stone, I got very excited, you know. To live that long four, five hundred years ago was unheard of."

"Aye."

He continued to speak, although she watched him carefully now. "Some of the grave stones looked so old…I've never seen such old stones in a graveyard. The carvings were completely worn away."

"I know those stones well," she said, her voice almost a whisper.

"You do?"

"Of course. The dead they mark are my own ancestors."

Ryan nodded, finding it hard to draw air into his lungs. "I'm sorry to have to tell you like this. But I really should."

She sat up straight on the duvet.

"I dug up—I mean, I excavated—one of your ancestor's graves," he blurted. "I didn't know it was your ancestor, for sure. But those dates…I couldn't get them out of my mind. I had to know."

The blanket slipped from her fingers, revealing her pink nipples. Her mouth opened slightly, her eyes squinted.

"I sent a bone off for genetic testing. To determine the age of the person buried in the grave."

He couldn't look at her face, his punishment for the pain he was causing her. "I also took a strand of Cleona's hair, for DNA testing. I should have asked you first, I know. But I need to ask you a favor...I need to get a sample from Catherine too. And from you, if you'll let me. It's just a cheek swab, you see, I've got a br---"

She stood up and the blanket fell away. "You never believed me," she said calmly, unconcerned with her nakedness. "Everything I told you."

"No! I believed you," he insisted, placing a firm hand on her foot. "I believed that *you* believed."

She pulled her foot out from his grip and stepped into her underwear. "You seemed to care about us, to want to understand."

"I do," he said. "I care about you very much. Being this close with someone, I mean, I've never..."

Ryan put his face into his hands, hands that still smelled of the thousands of unknown scents on Aisling's skin. He still couldn't say that he *believed* her.

"Fear and death drive you, not love," she said. "Not life."

He knew that she was right. Even when he was inside of her, the old bones in the graveyard, the Owen DNA, still haunted his thoughts.

"I could never leave this island." Tears ran down her flushed face, which disappeared from sight as she pulled the wool sweater over her head. "I was a fool to even think it."

Ryan made his way over to his pile of clothing and dressed, not caring that the buttons missed some of their holes.

"I don't want to leave," he said, his voice breaking. He reached his arms tightly around her torso, pulled her close to him, but she pushed him away.

"You don't belong here," she said sadly.

He hung his head, and she stepped into the lower room. He gathered his things slowly, and when he shut the door to the cottage, he felt that he was closing the door on his *own* story, which was only just now beginning.

15

Mother Superior sat beside Sister Ignatius in Dorothy O'Sullivan's crusted car, and Sister Charlotte—the only novitiate in the small, greying convent—sat erectly in the front seat. Sister Charlotte wasn't even bound to take a male or even a female saint's name, so lax were the standards of orders nowadays.

Bespectacled Mother Superior, almost 80 years old, was the only other nun in the convent who could identify Sister Ambrose; when Sister Ignatius had called her from the telephone in her hotel room and told her what she'd discovered, Mother Superior had tenderly voiced her doubt. But Sister Ignatius had begged her to come, to see for herself, and Mother Superior had agreed to visit.

The file that Mother Superior had found in the convent archives—a grey folder containing articles about Sister Ambrose's disappearance from two Irish newspapers and some handwritten notes—rested in a tote bag in the space between them.

"I don't want to nose around in your affairs, but it *is* curious to me, you sisters comin' to see the old woman," said Dorothy. "And the Yank too. Sure but he seems fascinated with the lot of them."

The nuns remained silent as they surveyed the scenery—green with the recent infusion of moisture—beyond the windows.

"I don't suppose you'd like to give me a hint," teased Dorothy. "The Yank won't say a word to me about his business. He claims to be some kind of scientist, but I'm not so sure. He's shifty, that one."

Mother Superior sighed. The car nosed its way up a steep incline, and the engine whined in protest.

Dorothy turned around, keeping one hand on the steering wheel. "It's just that some think she's a witch," she said merrily.

"Did you know that the word *witch* comes from the Saxon word for *wise one*?" Mother Superior asked.

Dorothy blinked, then turned to face the road, just as the Peugeot careened into a pothole. Her brooding silence was like a fifth passenger for the remainder of the trip, and when she dropped them at Catherine's cottage, she muttered about returning in an hour to get them, then screeched away.

Mother Superior knocked on the door, and Sister Ignatius said, "She won't answer."

Crossing herself, Mother Superior opened the door, and the nuns filed inside.

Sister Ambrose still slept in the bed. They stepped quietly across the earthen floor to her side. Mother Superior bent down and pulled the file from the tote bag. She opened the grey folder, and Sister Ignatius could see the yellowed newspaper articles, cut from a larger sheet of newsprint dated June 6, 1950.

Mother Superior held the article close to her face, then examined the newspaper photograph. The woman in the photo was elderly, but her eyes shone with good health, even in black and white.

Mother Superior looked from the photograph in the article to the woman in the bed. She stared at them both for a long time, her eyes huge behind the thick glasses. She beckoned the younger nun to make her own examination. She too gazed at the photo, then at the woman in the bed. The nuns looked to one another then, and barely shook their heads.

"Sister Ignatius," Mother Superior whispered. Her lips trembled.

"What are you sayin'?" Sister Ignatius tried not to speak too loudly.

"This woman is not Sister Ambrose. You...you made a mistake."

Sister Ignatius's head throbbed, the dreary room spun. "Aye, it is," she rasped. "Look again, for God's sake! The face underneath all those spots and wrinkles is one and the same!"

They didn't even look. They only stared at Sister Ignatius with careful eyes.

"No, sister. It's your mind gone astray. You can't help it," said Mother Superior.

Sister Ignatius grabbed the newspaper article and shoved it under the nose of Sister Charlotte. "Look! It's her! It's plain to the eye!"

Sister Charlotte shook her head. "I don't believe it is. I'm sorry. It's just not possible."

"Aye, it's not possible! But it's happened!"

"Time to go, sister," said Mother Superior softly. She put a hand on Sister Ignatius's arm and tried to lead her from the bedside, but Sister Ignatius shrugged her off. Sister Charlotte was only a novitiate, a novitiate with her baptismal name no less. She wore a shorter veil, and she hadn't even taken her final vows yet.

Sister Ignatius stared at the face above the blankets. Her throat sticky with tears, she said, "I want to say my goodbyes."

Mother Superior nodded once, and she and Sister Charlotte walked quietly to the front door.

"Sister Ambrose," she whispered. The tears dripped into her mouth. "It's me, Evie O'Grady. Sister Ignatius."

Her body shook as she prayed to God aloud. She sang a hymn, very softly. To her surprise, the woman moaned, shifted her fuzzy head on the flattened pillow.

Sister Ignatius leaned over her. She could barely hear the whispers coming from Sister Ambrose's cracked mouth. "My sister," she said.

A hot tear fell onto the woman's folded hands. "Aye, that's right. I'm Sister Ignatius," she encouraged.

Sister Ambrose opened her eyes to gaze at Sister Ignatius. Sister Ignatius believed that she could hear the clouds parting in the sky, and she was back in the sun-filled garden with Sister Ambrose, and she was young, spirited and stubborn. The skin of her hands was opaque, the netted hair beneath the coif a glossy black.

Sister Ignatius grabbed the woman's cold, bony fingers and squeezed them tightly. "I know it's you, Sister Ambrose. I'm here for you."

Suddenly, Mother Superior was beside her again. She took

Sister Ignatius's upper arm with a firm grip, as if she were about to collapse. But Sister Ignatius didn't feel unsteady at all.

"It's her, I know it is," she whimpered. "God wants you to believe me."

She shut her eyes, blocking out the sight of her fellow sisters, their faces of pity.

16

———————

Ryan still stood outside Aisling's cottage, silent since his departure a half-hour ago. The dark, grey clouds still lingered. The wind was blowing, thick with salt, and the temperature was chilly enough for a coat. The vast ocean beyond the cliffs was a menace, with jagged white-caps scattered over the navy blue swells.

He shivered in his long-sleeved cotton shirt and khaki pants, his funeral attire. He watched the sky shift its colors with every second; he heard the seabirds cry, mourning the arrival of winter. It was time to atone.

After a while, he heard the door to Catherine's cottage creak open. From behind his dirty glasses lens, he saw three nuns emerge from the front door. Their faces, one young and two old, were somber. He recognized the nun that had checked on him that night, and as he stared, she soon turned to him.

"You're here for the miracle, aren't you?" she called, her voice clear, despite her frail appearance.

The other nuns' eyes shifted nervously, and they moved closer to the nun who had spoken.

"I am." A couple of drops of cold rain fell on Ryan's head.

The nuns continued to stare at him as the wind whipped their habits around their legs, revealing sensible black shoes beneath. Soon, he heard the rumble of an old car approaching. The green Peugeot stopped in front of Catherine's cottage, and Ryan saw Dorothy O'Sullivan through the windshield. The wipers made a screeching noise as they wiped away the beginnings of the rain.

The nuns got into the car as Dorothy rolled the window down. "Look what the cat dragged in. I was getting' worried, so," she scolded him. "Do you need a ride back?"

"Looks like your car is already full," he called.

"It wouldn't be the first time that someone's ridden along on the bonnet," she said. She reached out and patted the wet hood. "Jump on, then."

"No thanks. I'll walk."

"In the rain?"

"I don't mind it."

She said something like "Americans" to the nuns and rolled the window back up. The nun who had spoken watched him from the back window until Dorothy made a slow U-turn in the road, tires grinding the rocks underneath, and inched back down the road.

∞

Ryan jogged along behind the car, down the muddy road, as giant circles of rain pelted his face.

When Dorothy maneuvered the car into an oil-stained spot near the shed, he saw the nuns, bearing black umbrellas, hurry from the car into the front parlor. The familiar nun, however, said a stern goodbye to them and walked into the back door of the hotel. He followed at a bit of a distance as she limped down the hall and opened the door to her room, right next to his own.

Ryan strode quickly up to her, as the rain dripped down his clothing to the thin runner on the floor.

"I'm Ryan Abernathy, from America," he blurted.

She turned, not surprised to find him there.

"I'm involved in a study of genetics and longevity, and I came here to speak with Cleona and Catherine about their ages. Unfortunately, Cleona passed before I was able to talk to her. And I don't think Catherine is able to talk to me. She seems in very bad shape."

She eyed him, her face tinged with yellow, the pouches of skin beneath her eyes smudged with gray. "Aye, that she is."

"Do you have a minute to speak with me, Sister...?"

"Sister Ignatius. Come in," she said, holding out the door for him. "I'll fetch you a towel."

He removed his filthy shoes and entered the hotel room, decorated in a similar fashion as his room, with religious paintings on faded wallpaper and outdated furniture, heavily nicked. The nun returned from the bathroom with a white towel, the same kind of towel he'd wrapped the old bone in.

She seated herself in the one upholstered armchair, while Ryan stood, rubbing his hair and wiping down his clothing. She massaged her head for a few moments, then looked up at him with tired gray eyes.

"So you're a scientist of some kind?"

"I'm a geneticist. I study the genes and DNA of centenarians, mostly those of centenarian siblings."

"And why do you do this?"

"To further the knowledge of longevity. There is a genetic component to the clustering of extreme longevity in families, and I need to know how all of the genetic sequences work with one another. I hope to create certain therapies—pharmaceuticals, nutraceuticals, or compounds—that would enhance the average person's ability to prevent or treat age-related diseases and live longer lives."

Sister Ignatius shook her head. "So much science! I didn't understand the half of what you just said."

"Well, yes. That's what longevity comes down to."

"I can see why you received that beating," she sighed. She looked toward the rain-splattered window, which gave a clear view of the church. "Do you not believe that God has something to do with long life as well?"

"God...well, no, actually," he said apologetically. He shivered in his damp clothing.

"A higher power," she continued. "Behind your science."

"I wish that I did." He rubbed his hands up and down his arms. "I don't feel that there is anything watching over us. The world feels empty to me."

The nun looked through him. "Except when you're here, on the island."

He shrugged. Then he slowly began to nod.

"I feel the same, as it is," she said. "For a long time, I didn't feel that God cared for women as He did for men. I felt that women were forsaken, lesser, in His eyes. But He was helpin' me the whole time. I was led here, I'm sure of it."

The nun's eyes burned brightly, almost with fever.

"You knew Catherine, didn't you?" he asked.

"Aye," she said. Then she moaned softly and began rubbing her head again. Then she doubled over in the chair. She began to sob quietly.

Ryan hurried into the bathroom, searched for a glass, and filled it with the chlorinated water from the tap. He wished that he could offer her the clean water from the stream as he handed the glass to her.

"Here's some water, if you need it."

She looked up at the glass, then reached for it with a trembling hand. She drank sloppily, spilling some on her habit.

"I'm sorry," she breathed. "I'm not feeling well a-tall."

"Is there anything I can get you? I have some supplements in my bag."

She shook her head. "I have a brain tumor. My symptoms are gettin' worse by the day."

"Oh. I'm very sorry."

He thought briefly of his mother, the mutated cells inside her body unable to stop dividing. It was terrible to imagine the damage that a cancer in the brain could wreak.

Sister Ignatius tried to sit up straight. She spoke in a soft voice. "I knew Sister Ambrose—Catherine—for a brief time when she was a nun in our convent. She disappeared one day, and she was 119 years old at the time. The sisters worried about her for many years afterward."

She reached for a grey folder on the table beside her. "I have Mother Superior's file on her, as it happens."

She handed Ryan the folder, and he opened it to find several local newspaper articles and pages of handwritten notes. He read the articles first, most of which told of Sister Ambrose's disappearance from the convent.

She had been covered in the Irish newspapers four times before she disappeared, due to the convent's claim of the nun's extreme age; Ireland believed her to be the world's oldest woman, but apparently there was no documentation to support the claim, so the rest of the world disregarded it.

The first time an article had been written was in 1932, when Sister Ambrose had turned 100. The convent had organized a party for her in a garden on the large monastery's property; an accompanying photo showed a bright-eyed, elderly nun standing in a garden of daffodils, hands hidden in the sleeves of her habit.

Three more sets of articles focused on the nun's subsequent milestone birthdays, when she'd turned 105, 110 and then 115. Sister Ambrose appeared to have hardly aged a day in the photos that showed her gardening, singing, and working in the kitchen.

When she disappeared from the monastery, the newspapers ran a photograph of Sister Ambrose, a nun who in 1951 finally appeared extremely elderly. She looked somewhat similar to Catherine Owen, but the photo was in black and white, the paper yellowed and thin with age. The habit's veil encased a good portion of her face, which hung with wrinkled skin. It was impossible to equate the elderly nun in the photo with the decrepit Catherine Owen.

The articles detailed how the search had extended throughout the entire community—volunteers searched alleys and rivers and parks and churches, and police checked buses and cars and boat harbors in nearby towns—but no one ever found a trace of her.

A final article, written two weeks later, quoted the police detective: "We assume that Sister Ambrose wandered off during the night, without her wits, and has been a victim of foul play or a terrible accident." A reward had still been offered for any information leading to her whereabouts.

He then read the notes, taken by the Mother Superior at the time. It was a list of quotes from the sisters in the convent.

"Sister Ambrose is just like my granny—I don't think she's all there, but she is very sweet. She liked sheep, and she knit very well, as you know. I think she grew up on a farm."

"She talked wistfully of the ocean. I think she grew up near the sea, but I'm not sure."

"She told me once that she had taught herself to read the Bible in English."

"I heard her mumbling in her sleep sometimes. It was always in Gaelic. Yet, she claimed that she didn't speak Gaelic anymore, that she'd forgotten it."

"I think she had family somewhere. She didn't miss them very much, I guess, or she'd have written."

"She seemed to have secrets." I asked her to elaborate. *"I don't know what kind of secrets, but she kept a lot of things to herself. She never told me her place of birth. She never received letters or even wrote them. She must have had an unhappy childhood, or her family must all be dead. Perhaps she's just sad. I love Sister Ambrose very much."*

"She was the most devoted sister in the convent. She had little tolerance for superstitious pagans. She would never leave the

convent of her own free will. Someone—perhaps a Protestant— must have done something to her."

"The sisters are so very sad these days. We have lost a loved one, and we are in mourning. I hope the convent can survive this tragedy."

Ryan was struck by how little the nuns really knew of the disappeared sister. He looked up at Sister Ignatius, who had her eyes closed. The cancer was manifested in her skin, her eyes, even her breath.

"So no birth certificate for Sister Ambrose was ever produced," he said. "No records that the convent found that could corroborate its claims."

"No, I don't believe so. We just had faith."

Ryan let out a long, whistling breath. "If this Sister Ambrose is Catherine Owen, she would be the oldest person—by almost sixty years—ever recorded in the history of man."

"Sister Ambrose is approximately 180 years old."

He squeezed his eyes shut, and thought of Aisling with guilty pain. Then he looked down at the photographs of Sister Ambrose and Catherine Owen.

"It's a miracle," she declared defiantly. Her eyes were full of unshed tears. "Mother Superior doesn't believe me. She and Sister Charlotte came out here to fetch me away, back to the convent."

He flipped absently through the papers on his lap again. He wanted so desperately to believe. It made him uncomfortable to lead her on, and he got to his feet. He hoped the nuns would take her back to her convent tomorrow and get her some medical assistance. This island was obviously no place for her now.

She edged to the end of the chair. "What about you, Mr. Abernathy? You believe me, I know."

Ryan shuffled his feet and shrugged. "I haven't been able to get much concrete information."

He watched her eyes drift left and right as she thought. Her breath was shallow. "The news would bring a church to the island," she murmured. "A small, simple church facing the western sea."

Ryan quietly placed the folder on the table beside her.

"It could change the world. Bring the world back to religion, to God. It is what we have prayed for. God led me here, to the island, and it's no coincidence that our rooms are next door to each other, that I heard your cries that night. I was led here to find you too."

The tears in her eyes pooled thickly onto her cheeks.

"I'm dying," she said. "And before I die, I need to spread the word. For God. He has called on me, and I can't disappoint Him."

"Alright," he said soothingly. He was suddenly afraid that she was going to die, right there in front of him. "Whatever you need to do."

She breathed. "Thank you, Mr. Abernathy."

"I'm next door, if you need anything," he said, with a small smile. He slung his backpack over his shoulder.

∞

In his room, Ryan peeled off the wet clothes and hung them on the shower rod. He had fallen far behind in his studying, but the importance failed to energize him. He turned on the bedside lamp, for it was dark out now, even though it was only four in the afternoon. He stared at the bottle of medication on his bedside table; the little white pills waited to calm a distress that couldn't be ameliorated. He picked the bottle up and threw it against the dresser.

Then he got up and walked to the painting of the nun, still gazing morosely out at the world. The red door behind her head contrasted sharply with the black and white habit, with the green eyes of the nun.

Fully clothed, he got into the bed, listening to the rain rail against the slate roof. In the darkness, he drifted back to the cottage. He could remember exactly how the inside of Aisling's mouth had felt, the arrangement of her teeth.

His throat tightened so that he couldn't even swallow. He remembered this desolation; it was a small taste of what it would be like to be dead.

He turned off the lamp and curled into the weighty blankets, listening to the restless sounds of Sister Ignatius. At times it seemed that she had calmed down, perhaps gone to sleep, but then he would hear a drawer bang or a floorboard creak.

After some time, he heard a knock on her door and the sound of muffled conversation. Then the door closed, and he heard footsteps down the hall, most likely those of the other nuns. He heard the sound of pots banging and dishes clattering downstairs; he supposed it was nearing dinnertime, but he wasn't hungry.

Soon, he heard Sister Ignatius speaking in low tones, and figured that she was using the direct-dial telephone in her room. Her conversations, separated by brief silences, continued for at least two hours. It might have been longer, but sleep was pulling him under.

Just before he was lost to it, he pondered the possibility that he was close to a mystery of life. It was the way that Charles Darwin must have felt, when he realized that all species of life had descended over time from common ancestors. His theories, outlined in his 1859 book *On the Origin of Species*, were now basic information, beautiful in their simplicity.

17

The following morning Ryan awoke to the sound of loud, unfamiliar voices coming from the first floor of the hotel. The sun had barely risen. Somehow panicked, he dressed in the dark, grabbed his backpack and ventured down the stairs.

But just as he entered the front parlor, he saw a large group of well-dressed men and women walking out the front door. Three men, toting what looked to be cases containing television cameras, joined them outside. They boarded the dilapidated tour bus, and soon the vehicle chugged off down the main road toward the West Village. Before it left, however, Ryan saw a figure near the front—a figure that seemed to be wearing a veil and habit.

Ryan stared after the bus in a state of shock. The group of people were reporters, he knew. He smelled hairspray and cigarette smoke in their wake. The scent made him nauseous.

Wally's voice penetrated the ringing vacuum of thought. "Seems they've sniffed the story out, mate."

Ryan turned to see Wally, sitting in an armchair with a cup and saucer balanced on his knee.

"What story?" he asked, his voice cracking.

"Heard them say a bit about the old woman in the West Village," he said. "You know the one."

"And?" Ryan could hardly stand upright.

"They got a tip yesterday about her age. The nun, staying here in the..."

Ryan didn't wait for Wally to finish. He bolted out the door and galloped down the low road, riddled with rain-filled potholes. The achromatic clouds overhead promised more rain soon, and the wind flogged his hair, pinched his glasses into the bridge of his nose. The air had turned sharply colder, making him run all the harder.

He sprinted by the graveyard in a blur, and soon saw the familiar houses in a slope of hill ahead. And then he saw the group, congregated outside Catherine's cottage. Through the little crowd, he saw Sister Ignatius standing outside the door, her pale face raised with pride.

Ryan loped up the hill, aiming straight for the crowd. Cameras had already been removed from their cases and hoisted onto shoulders, and reporters called out to Sister Ignatius with spastic voices.

*"How old **is** she, sister?"*

"How do you know her? Is she a nun as well?"

"Does she have a twin?"

Sister Ignatius smiled indulgently. "If you'll just quiet down a moment, I'll tell you all you need to know. Then you can see her for yourselves."

"Wait," called Ryan, still breathless from the three-mile

sprint. He moved through the tangle of waving arms and microphones, and all of the frenzied faces turned towards him as he joined Sister Ignatius. He saw their breath in the frigid air.

As he turned to face the crowd, he saw Aisling emerge from the front door of her cottage. Her funereal black dress was wrinkled and hung sloppily over one shoulder, as if half-unzipped. Her hair tangled about her shoulders. She was barefoot.

"Here is the man that will corroborate the claim with science," said Sister Ignatius, patting his arm fondly.

The reporters' faces lit up with glee. "Name and occupation, please!" they yelled, notebooks and pens poised.

"I'm Ryan Abernathy, from the States. I'm a geneticist."

They murmured excitedly for a moment, the inclusion of science in the story apparently important to them.

"Why are you here, Mr. Abernathy? What have you found out about Catherine Owen?" asked a blonde Irish reporter with burgundy lipstick.

She shoved her microphone into his face. "Is she really the oldest woman in the world?"

Two more microphones were pushed toward his mouth, cameras aimed for his face.

Instead of answering immediately, Ryan's eyes flitted toward Aisling. *She was so beautiful*, he thought, standing there on the edge of her precarious world. She looked cold, and he wished she'd put the damned sweater on.

He laughed then and shook his head, as if the reporters were silly children. "I'm afraid Sister Ignatius has lured you here on false pretenses."

There was silence, as eyes flitted back and forth.

"What are you sayin'?" Sister Ignatius mumbled to him through pursed, blue lips.

Ryan spoke in a normal tone. "I'm saying that reaching the age you're claiming for Catherine Owen is impossible for a human being to do, sister."

She turned to the crowd, the hem of her habit whipping. "He's not tellin' you the truth. He wants to keep the story for himself, for *science*."

Her voice cut through the moist morning air. "That's why he's here. He wants DNA samples. He wants to make drugs that help people live forever. He wants to be rich and famous, it's plain to see."

Ryan turned towards Aisling, whose face was now obscured by her windblown hair. He didn't even think before he spoke.

"It's true that I came to the island to meet with Cleona and Catherine Owen. My research study received some information from a local doctor, who believed that the twin sisters were over 100 years old. He correctly assumed that this information would be intriguing to our study, because the genes of long-lived siblings, especially twins, help us tremendously in our quest to isolate so-called longevity genes so that we can figure out how they work in helping people live extremely long lives. So that we can help others—those of us without such impressive genes—live long and healthy lives as well."

He could feel Aisling's eyes watching him, but he refused to lose his train of thought. "Unfortunately, I haven't been able to determine their exact ages, for they don't have valid age documentation. It's been a bit of a wild goose chase, but it's nothing that the study hasn't seen before. We often investigate age claims, only to come away disappointed."

"Where is the twin?" a clean-cut male reporter called.

"Unfortunately, she passed away three days ago."

"What about their DNA?" asked an Asian male reporter. "Could their DNA tell you how old the surviving twin is?"

"DNA reveals many things...many wonderful things and many terrifying things... but unfortunately, it can't tell us the age of a body."

Sister Ignatius interrupted the reporters' sudden discussion. "Catherine Owen was a nun in my convent. I remember her very clearly. Sixty-two years ago she was 119 years old."

Ryan tried to compose himself. He asked for forgiveness, not from God necessarily, but from the generic universe.

"The nun here has brain cancer. She has been suffering from delusions and debilitating pain. She doesn't know what she's talking about. What's more, I've been told Catherine has advanced dementia. I doubt she can remember her own name."

"I have proof!" yelled Sister Ignatius. Her pale face was now bright red. "Photographic proof!"

The reporters again turned toward the nun, microphones poised. "Let's see it then!"

"I have a series of photos of Sister Ambrose, or Catherine Owen, as well as a photo that I took two days ago, here in this cottage."

She pulled the newspaper articles and a glossy four-by-six photo from a pocket in her habit and held them up in front of her with trembling hands. The reporters surged forward, pushing and shoving each other for a better view.

"You can see that the woman is quite elderly in the black-and-white photos."

She was silent while the reporters looked from photo to photo.

"She disappeared from the convent a few years after the photo was taken," read the blonde reporter. "She was believed to be 119 years old at the time."

The reporters scribbled in their notebooks, the cameras trained on the photos.

Sister Ignatius exclaimed, "And over 60 years later, I found her here, on the island. Living in this cottage, next to a twin biological sister we didn't know she had. *She is still alive.*"

The reporters gasped. The wind howled against the stone of the cottages.

"You see, Catherine Owen is touched by the hand of God. It's a miracle, so it is. It *is* still possible, even in these trying times."

The reporters stared at Sister Ignatius as they processed the information. Ryan thought that the nun sounded convincing; her voice was authoritative, almost priest-like. They then took in Ryan's face, his broken glasses, and he knew they were questioning his character. They murmured to one another.

Suddenly, a loud cracking of wood on rock broke through the cacophony. Ryan turned to see Murray, holding a giant club, stained with old blood, and relief flooded his limbs.

Murray called, "This family is in mournin', and you're bein' rude. Move along now, back to the filthy streets you came from. The show's over."

The reporters stared at Murray, looming like an ogre in the gray dawn. One of the stronger cameramen broke the silence. "We came to see about the old woman. We're not leavin' without the story."

Murray strode over to the cameraman, toting the club on his massive shoulder. "I don't believe I heard you."

The man backed up slightly. "I said we aren't goin' nowhere. The nun's told us the scoop, now we've got to get our interview. She promised us, and we've come a good ways to get here."

Murray raised the club high over his head and brought it down with an ear-splitting crack on the camera. "There's no law on the island. Did you know that?" he growled.

One of the female reporters screamed, and others began backing away from Murray.

Sister Ignatius quickly opened the door to Catherine's cottage and beckoned the crowd inside. The reporters and cameramen rushed for the door, as Murray and Ryan grabbed sleeves and collars and hoods. Aisling ran over, blindly grabbing the reporters' arms through her tears.

But no one could stop the wave of curiosity that had infested them. Ryan and Murray and Aisling tried to follow the crowd into the cottage, but there was no room for them.

The cottage was suddenly silent. Then Ryan heard anxious murmurs.

Soon, he saw Sister Ignatius part the crowd. Her face was whiter than Ryan had ever seen it.

First, she crossed herself. Then, to Aisling, she whispered, "She's passed on."

Ryan stood in the doorway, so he had no choice but to go back outside. And as he turned, he saw a red chip of paint, stuck deeply inside the worn wood of the door.

18

———————

Aisling fought down a wave of nausea as she stood on a chair and screwed a light bulb into the socket on the ceiling. She flipped the switch on the white-washed wall near the door, then smiled at the glow that the little bulb produced. The rush of light was timely, for it was Christmas morning.

Last night, instead of going to mass in the East Village, Aisling and Murray had stood beside the Yule log he'd brought her, an ancient symbol of life and death. They watched the gigantic log burn over an old piece of turf, filling the old cottage with light and warmth. For a brief moment, hope filled Aisling's heart, and she allowed herself to think of the future.

She had wanted the company of someone, so Murray had stuck around for a while. She'd knitted him a sweater, the dark blue of a stormy sea, but she'd thought only of Ryan's face as the yarn obeyed the needles, ultimately gathering into a complex pattern of wild beauty. It was the best sweater she'd ever knitted.

Murray had accepted the gift almost sheepishly, and hadn't

offered her anything in return but the Yule log. She could tell he'd wanted to meet his friends at the pub for some Christmas Eve celebrating. On his way out the door, Murray had tried to kiss her—on her cheek—but a wave of nausea had overtaken her, and she had closed the door on him.

He didn't know about the pregnancy yet.

As she carefully sipped her hot tea, she thought of the dream that she'd had last night. Again a corncrake, she guarded a nest containing one egg; yet still she cried for her mate, over and over again, for she was afraid of the approaching mower. She never received a response, even though she'd cried until she was hoarse. She had awoken with a sore throat and tears on her face, the cottage cold as death and the rain leaking through the roof onto the quilt on Cleona's bed.

She had layed there, trying to imagine the future, a story she didn't know until she lived it herself.

As she was finishing her tea, she heard a knock on the door. Then, before she could get up, the door squeaked open and through the slit she saw the bright blonde hair of Kiley against the dark sepia of the morning.

"*Nollaig shona*!" cried Kiley.

Aisling jumped up and threw the door wide open as Kiley jumped to her, her skinny arms tight around Aisling's back. The loneliness rose up through her gut like the winter wind.

"I'm sorry for Cleona and Catherine," Kiley moaned.

She reeked of perfume, and her face was plastered with every available kind of makeup. "I wanted to come for the services, but I didn't have the money. I've been savin' for the holiday, you know."

"It's alright," said Aisling, touching her friend's face with both of her hands. Kiley's eyes were still a lively blue beneath the black lines and lashes. "I'm just happy to see you!"

Kiley's eyes swept the cottage. "Not a thing has changed, I see. You still sleep in the loft?"

"Aye." She certainly wasn't going to sleep in Cleona's bed, and her loft was tolerable, even in the winter.

"I'll bet Murray's been keepin' you company up there," Kiley said, a wicked grin on her face.

She strolled into the cottage and removed her leather jacket, revealing a tight pink t-shirt, through which Aisling could see a black brassiere. She poured herself some tea from the kettle.

"Isn't it strange without them? You must be mighty lonely."

"Aye." She followed Kiley about the cottage, afraid she would vanish, a figment of her loosened imagination.

Kiley sipped her tea as she regarded Aisling. "You haven't aged a day, girl," she marveled. She reached out and stroked Aisling's cheek. "It's not natural. You look younger than a teenager."

"You look good…" said Aisling.

"Oh, give over, will you. I did get a new tattoo." She pulled back her sleeve to reveal a small black seal on the inside of her wrist. "You know how you used to tell me all those selkie stories? I thought they were stupid fairy tales, you know, but they snuck up on me in Dublin of all places."

She kissed her tattoo, leaving a red lipstick print on top of the seal.

Kiley ran her fingers through Aisling's hair, glossy and even thicker with pregnancy. "I've showed your photograph to all of my boyfriends, and they all want to meet you. It's time for you to take a trip to Dublin."

"I can't do that."

Kiley groaned. "What nonsense are you talkin'? You really need to get yourself out of here. There's nothin' here for you anymore."

Aisling slumped into a chair. "Kiley, I'm pregnant."

Kiley dropped her tea cup on the dirt floor. "Holy Mary," whispered Kiley.

"It's early yet."

"So you finally got your monthlies, did you?" Her voice was breathless.

"Aye."

Kiley sat down slowly across from Aisling. "Is it Murray's, then?"

"No."

"Who?" she asked incredulously. "Who's the da?"

"An American man. He came here a month and a half ago, wantin' to talk with Cleona and Catherine about their ages. He's a scientist."

Aisling's growing breasts tingled at the mention of Ryan, who seemed more and more like a man she'd made up.

"Sounds like he wanted to do more than talk to old ladies," said Kiley.

Aisling put her hands in front of her face and smiled.

"What did he want with them?"

"Somethin' about their genes, about them bein' twins. He wanted to figure out what it was made them so old."

"So he just up and left you after gettin' you with child?"

"I wanted him gone."

"Why?"

Aisling paused, unsure how to explain it all to Kiley. "He

didn't understand me, my life here. On the island."

"Neither do I!" spluttered Kiley. "Doesn't mean he's not fit for you."

"He's off his nut," said Aisling. "He dug up my ancestor's bone from the graveyard! Stole a strand of Cleona's hair from her dead body!"

Kiley suddenly laughed. "I like the sound of him."

"What do you think I should do? What would you do?"

Kiley just shook her head, messed up her hair with both hands as she thought. Finally she said, "The baby needs a da. Just as you did. Remember?"

Aisling nodded. She'd missed out on holding her da's hand, sitting on his knee, watching him as he fished with his crew on the wild seas. She'd grown up with the island as her teacher, alone but for Cleona's stories.

Aisling saw Ryan, the day that he'd stood outside Catherine's cottage and spoken to the reporters. His hair had flown wildly backwards, revealing his battered face. He had kept looking over at her, all of the closeness from the days before blowing in the wind between them. He'd stood there on the threshold of Catherine's cottage as a kind of guardian. She had seen the truth of him, but she hadn't realized it then.

Kiley opened her big black bag with a sequined dragon on it and pulled out a bottle of gold nail polish and two tubes of lipstick. "I brought you some presents. This golden color is popular in Dublin right now."

She held the bottle to Aisling's hand. "I thought it would look smart next to these freckles."

"It's beautiful," said Aisling.

She jumped up and grabbed the light blue scarf from the

knitting basket. "I know it's not fancy, but I carded and spun the wool myself. Somethin' to keep you warm in Dublin this winter."

Kiley fingered the scarf, then wrapped it around her neck. It matched her eyes. "I'll think of you every time I wear it. You and your wee one." She patted Aisling's stomach.

Kiley then turned and lifted her black leather jacket from the back of the chair. "And I wanted you to have this."

The jacket sat heavily on Aisling's lap. "No, Kiley. I couldn't. You've had it forever."

"I know," she said. "But I bought another one with my discount at the shop where I'm workin' on the weekends. I don't need two leather jackets, now."

Kiley stood up and grabbed the jacket, holding it out for Aisling. "Try it on."

Aisling grinned and slipped her arms into the jacket. She zipped it up, smelled the faint perfume that lingered in the collar. The jacket was buttery and warm.

"I doubt it'll zip up when your belly starts growin'," teased Kiley.

"Even so," said Aisling dreamily. "I'm never takin' it off."

"Just like those jeans you're wearin'," noted Kiley. "You need a new pair, girl. Those patches are pathetic."

Aisling had finally patched the holes in the knees with two old pieces of thick, red felt.

"Don't you dare spend any more of your money on me."

Kiley began applying some lipstick to Aisling's lips. "Not that you need any of this shite, with this fairy face. But these full lips are just beggin' for a bit of color. There."

Kiley fished a cosmetic mirror from her shoulder bag and

held it up to Aisling's face.

Aisling saw a strange woman in the mirror, with blood-red lips, and she looked away.

"You don't like it," Kiley stated.

"I've just never worn makeup before." She disliked the waxy feel, the toxic taste of her lips.

"You don't need it." Kiley scooped up the lipstick tubes and put them back in her own bag. She leaned back and looked searchingly at Aisling.

"Are you scared?" asked Kiley. "Because of what happened to your mam and all?"

"Aye."

"You should see a doctor, Aisling. I'll take you tomorrow, while I'm still here." She hugged Aisling tightly. "My da's been tryin' to get me to give him some money for the pub, the drouth! It'll be grand to get away from him for a bit."

"I'm sure he misses you," said Aisling. "This island isn't the same without you."

∞

The next morning, Aisling and Kiley took the ferry to the mainland. Then they walked the four miles to the doctor's office, the way Aisling had done when she'd needed help for Cleona and Catherine.

She had liked Dr. Fitzgerald, one of the only doctors around. He had made the crossing immediately, no questions asked. He wasn't good-looking, but he was kind and wouldn't let her pay him, even though all she could offer him was a hand-knit sweater. He had treated Catherine and Cleona with respect, even though he was too curious about their ages. And he kept a photo of his wife and three children on his desk. Aisling had made up stories about the happy-looking family for days afterward.

As they walked, Kiley told Aisling all about Dublin life, making it sound as good as *Tír na nÓg*. They stopped at a market for Kiley to buy some cigarettes, and the cashier stared at Aisling so much that she gave Kiley too much change. On their way out the door, Aisling saw the woman cross herself.

Back on the road, Aisling and Kiley shared a cigarette. "I don't like it here," Aisling said. "Everyone stares at me."

"And here I was thinkin' they were all starin' at *me*!" jeered Kiley. "And my new boots, of course." The fringe along the tops of her black suede boots rippled violently with her quick stride.

After an hour of walking and talking, they reached the doctor's office. There were only two other people in the waiting room, so Kiley and Aisling took seats next to one another. Kiley immediately snatched up a fashion magazine, but Aisling rifled through the stack aimlessly. Then she found a book, nestled in the basket of children's toys.

On the cover, in English, were the words "Irish Fairy Tales." The book was filled with pictures, which helped her along with the words, but she found the whole book quite boring, no match for Cleona's tales. After an hour and a half, a nurse popped her head out of the door and called Aisling's name.

"What is it you're seein' the doctor for today?" asked the nurse, once they were in the examination room.

"She's pregnant," said Kiley.

"Oh, how lovely," said the nurse to Aisling. "How far along are you?"

"About two months," said Kiley.

The nurse eyed Kiley's boots. "Where's the father?"

"Just send in the doc," growled Kiley.

"You'll have to remove your jeans and underwear," the nurse said to Aisling. "And lay that sheet over you." She turned on her heel and left the room.

"You're going to have to let me talk," said Aisling.

"I am!" cried Kiley.

The doctor came in, looking at a clipboard. Then he looked up and smiled. He was short, and his eyes twinkled. "Aisling! How nice to see you again."

Kiley stood up and stuck out her hand, bangles jingling. "I'm Kiley MacSheehan, doctor. Lifelong friend of Aisling's."

"Another island lass," he said, shaking her hand firmly. "My wife wants a summer home there, but I can't seem to make up my mind. I suppose you live on the mainland now."

"Where else would I live?" said Kiley.

"Well, your friend here seems to want to stay," he pointed out. "But now I see she's expecting a baby. Maybe she'll leave after all."

"I hope there's a truth in that, doctor," said Kiley.

He instructed Aisling to lie back on the table. "I was sorry to hear about your great-grandmother and her sister," he said softly, pushing on her slight belly with two warm hands. "I thought they were in bad shape, but I didn't want to scare you. I could see how much you cared about them."

She couldn't talk, with him touching her like that. She closed her eyes and thought only of Ryan's shy hands, their clean nails.

"You're still in the first trimester, but I'm going to have to examine your uterus," he said, looking at Kiley. "You'll probably want to leave for this."

"Aye," she agreed. Kiley kissed Aisling on the cheek and left in a haze of perfume, different than the previous day's scent.

He told Aisling to bend her legs and spread them far apart while he snapped some latex gloves onto his hands. She squeezed her eyes shut at the sight of him between her legs. He then slipped a cold metal device inside her, and she gasped as it seemed to spread her wide open.

"Sorry," he said kindly.

After a few moments, he removed the device and Aisling sat up.

"Everything looks good," he said, removing the gloves and tossing them in a trash can. He hadn't even asked about the father.

"My mam..." she began. "She died while birthing me. And she birthed several dead babies before me."

He nodded, then wrote something down on the clipboard. "So you're worried the same thing will happen to you?"

She nodded, stroking her belly without realizing it.

"Not necessarily," he said. "Did she have adequate medical care while pregnant? Was she on a vitamin regimen?"

"I don't think so," she said. "Cleona acted as midwife."

"Did she?" he asked curiously. "Well, sometimes island midwives aren't as familiar with modern medicine. Proper medical care is important, Aisling. I'll give you some prenatal vitamins—you need the folic acid, especially right now. And you can come to see me, once a month. Bring me some of those sweaters you knit. I'll sell them to my friends."

"Really?"

"Sure," he said. "It would be an honor. I'm going to boast that I delivered the great-great-grand-baby of a centenarian. Just imagine the life this baby will have."

Aisling bit her lip, a picture of Cleona holding her baby on her lap. It hurt to think of what the baby would miss, but then, Aisling always had the stories.

"Which reminds me," continued the doctor. "I contacted a longevity study in the States, after meeting Cleona and Catherine. I hope you don't mind?"

Asling quickly shook her head.

"They said they'd send someone out to the island to take DNA samples, but I've been so busy, you know, I've lost track of just everything lately. Did they ever send someone?"

"Yes, he was here for several days."

Her words barely trickled from her mouth. She recalled the moment she had met him, how the sight of his earnest face had filled her with longing, how badly she'd wanted him to stay. "But they died during his visit, you know. And they never had any certificates or anything."

"That's a pity," said Dr. Fitzgerald. "I thought for sure he could obtain some DNA samples. The women seemed like world record holders to me. But what do I know? I'm just a local country doctor."

This doctor meant well, she thought. She was glad she had come.

∞

On their way into the harbor, Aisling spotted Murray walking down the pier toward land. His nets and gear were slung over his shoulder. She called out his name, and he jerked his head toward the sound.

She waved to him, but he just stood there staring, his dark eyes visible even from the punt. Then he started walking up to the road.

Kiley whistled low. "Is he mad with you? About the baby?"

"He doesn't know."

"Only a matter of time, girl."

Once she was back on land, Aisling said goodbye to Kiley and walked quickly down the road after him. "Murray!" she shouted.

He turned, just barely, and kept plodding along.

"What's wrong with you?" Her breath was a tiny cloud in the cold air between them.

He shrugged. She saw that he wore the sweater she'd given him for Christmas. "Where are you headin'?" she asked.

"Pub."

"I'll go with you."

He snorted. Women weren't encouraged to drink in the pub, even if it was empty of men and they were drinking water. Nevertheless, she followed Murray into the dark pub and seated herself on a stool next to Murray.

Donal blinked at Aisling for a moment, but as he fetched her a pint and placed it in front of her, he winked.

"On the house," he declared. The islanders had warmed up to her a bit more after Catherine's funeral, but she was still getting used to it.

"Hey Donal, how come you aren't offerin' up pints to me?" called Murray.

"Last time I checked, you weren't a fine-lookin' lassie."

Murray cut his eyes at Aisling's pint, then took a big swig from his own. Aisling took a sip of beer and felt her belly squirm. It occurred to her that she might have to give up beer for a while.

They sat in silence for a long time, as men streamed into the pub. When they caught sight of Aisling at the bar, they suddenly stopped talking, took on a false politeness. Aisling saw Kiley's father among them, skinny and with thinning blonde hair, smiling and easy. She guessed that Kiley had given him some money.

Murray finished his beer and motioned Donal for another. When Donal put the beer down in front of Murray, he said, "Don't be forgettin' that you owe me for a new fiddle."

Murray sighed.

"What happened to the other one?" Aisling asked.

"Well, my girl, he broke it, and that was a very old fiddle too, so it was. Was me granddad's, and he played it 'til the strings nearly broke," said Donal. "So are you goin' to play it or what?"

"You've got a new one already?" asked Murray.

"So I have, and waitin' on you to play her. No one else this time o' year can do the job."

He retreated behind the bar and pulled out a dusty, black case. Murray opened it and removed the gleaming, copper fiddle, a thing of beauty in the gloomy pub. He struck it with the bow, then tuned it a bit. Aisling could feel the men gathering around them. Kiley's father declared that he was buying everyone a round, and the men let out howls of happiness. She knew the joy as well, for she hadn't heard Murray play the fiddle in years.

It was quiet in the pub, then, as Murray began to sing in a rough yet melodic voice.

> *Oh! Calm was the lake of Coolfin on that day,*
> *When over its wide waters we glided along,*
> *No cloud in the heavens over shadowed our way,*

And light-hearted laughter was joined in our song.

The wild winds of winter now sweep over the lake,
The snowdrift lies deep on its desolate shore,
The roll of the thunder its echoes awake,
And summer time smiles on its bosom no more.

Murray's eyes closed now, and his arm worked the fiddle with a passion that belied its accustomed use as a fisherman's appendage. His voice sounded strange to her in its tenderness.

As bright is the sunshine of youth's early day,
As gay are the pleasures our life may begin;
In this world below they must soon pass away,
And be overcast as the lake of Coolfin.

Murray carefully lowered the fiddle and bow to his lap.

∞

"That's the way of it, sure," muttered Kiley's father.

"True enough for it," said another.

Aisling turned on the stool to see the men about her, their faces transformed from defeated, rugged masks to visages more thoughtful, perhaps even hopeful, despite the sad tenor of the song. The men patted Murray on the back, and one bought him a shot of whiskey.

"That was some mighty powerful playin' there, Murray," said Donal. "You could have picked a friskier tune, though, if you don't mind me sayin'."

"These are not such frisky times, are they, Donal?" said Murray.

"That's my point now, isn't it?"

The music and the men brought back a memory of a time long ago, when she'd just lost her father. A girl of only five years, she'd come to the window of the pub, where the men had gathered after the funeral. They played songs like that one, and told stories of his life on the sea, of his love for her mother and for his young daughter, things that even Cleona had never told her, not in so many simple words. The pub had seemed a magical place then; perhaps it still was.

She thought of Cleona and Catherine and all of her ancestors, whose faces she didn't know but whose characters she did. But most of all, she thought of Ryan Abernathy. She wondered if he even thought about her, swallowed by the land of plenty. America—with Indiana corn and DNA and McDonald's —was even more unknowable than the Otherworld.

She couldn't see herself anywhere else but on the island.

The men scattered about the pub once again, talking merrily amongst themselves. A haze of tobacco smoke thickened the air. Murray put the fiddle and bow into the case and slowly snapped it shut, as if his fingers pained him.

"My brother's got some work for me on an offshore whitefish fleet," he said to his glass. "I start next week, and I won't be comin' back here for a while. He's based on the coast up north, you know."

"Oh," she said, the air gone from her lungs, the loneliness replacing it. "Well, good for you, Murray. You'll be makin' a pretty penny, won't you?"

"Aye," he admitted. "That'll be a change."

"Don't go spendin' it all in the pubs, now."

He turned his body to her, but he couldn't look her in the eye. "I'll send some for you."

Ailsing shook her head. "Don't."

"It's either that or the dole, girl." She watched as a gulp of beer moved down his throat.

"Murray, I'm pregnant."

He was motionless, his empty glass wavering in the air. "The scientist?" he whispered.

"Aye."

"Does he know?" Anger simmered on Murray's face, a look she'd seen many times before.

"No."

"Are you plannin' on tellin' him?" The tenor of his voice caused the other men in the pub to look over. Donal refilled his glass.

"Aye," she said softly. "Soon."

He nodded. Then he screwed up his face, so that it matched his broken nose. "Used some fairy magic on him, didn't you?"

"What are you sayin'?" Her heart pounded in her chest, wanting out. She put a hand over it.

"The man was struck dumb by the sight of you," he said, his eyebrows now one long black line. He leaned closer to her ear. "I know about you, girl. I know about your family. I always have."

"Murray..." Tears sprung to her eyes.

"I've got to get out from under you. That's why I'm leavin'," he said, his eyes full of tears.

He stood up and threw some money down on the bar. Then he left without another word to her. The pub was silent, and she could feel the men staring at her back. She gulped down the rest

of her beer and then walked out of the pub into a windless
downpour of rain.

19

———

One month after returning from Ireland, Ryan leaned over his kitchen table, a laptop, papers and books spread in front of him. His cheekbone still resembled a rotting avocado, but the swelling in his lip had completely receded. His head bore a tiny, stubborn lump that still yipped when he brushed his hair.

But Ryan hardly looked into a mirror, not even to shave. He moved through the days with little enthusiasm. It was the hilltop graveyard, and how Aisling had appeared standing amongst the stones, that now occupied his thoughts, not the bones or the DNA inside them.

At the news of Catherine's death, the crowd had somberly filed out of the cottage and climbed back onto the tour bus with little fanfare. Saddened, Ryan had left Aisling, crying in the muscled arms of Murray. Ryan had quietly packed his dirty clothes and left the island on a ferry the following morning. He didn't remember dropping off his rental car, or the flight back to America.

Now, he gazed about him, seeing things in a new light. His apartment was a sad, sterile excuse for a domicile. Not even a houseplant drew oxygen there; no germs would dare proliferate on its surfaces. The tidiness exuded loneliness, and the impressive stacks of academic books had no answers at all. His vegetables and fruit were defeated, gelatinous blobs.

His treadmill gathered dust, for he now preferred to run outside, past the street's lines of pine and bare cedar trees. He had tossed his bottles of supplements in the trash the minute he'd gotten home, and the feeling of natural health had kept him from veering to depression.

He drank black tea; he purchased incense that smelled of Irish turf smoke; he found a book in the library about Celtic mythology. He even rented several movies that took place in Ireland and spent days watching them, over and over. But nothing brought back the warmth of the fire, the downiness of Aisling's unshaven legs, the feeling that he had found his family.

He still had the strand of Cleona's hair in an envelope, but it was now stuffed in his sock and underwear drawer, underneath his most ragged boxers. And the painting of the nun sat on his bedside table. It was the last thing he looked at before going to sleep at night.

Rose fretted over the box, still in mail limbo, but Ryan hardly cared. It was just a bone, a mere remnant of a living human being. Nothing more.

∞

In the library, he searched for books about the islands off the western coast of Ireland, but he didn't have much luck. He ended up ordering a dozen, more obscure books from the internet, most of which were written by western island locals in the late nineteenth century.

He took his time reading through them, silently thanking Wally Rose for encouraging him in the endeavor. Mostly memoirs, they detailed a hard, isolated life of fishing and farming that most people now shunned.

He was reading a chapter in a compilation of old letters, written by an island man to his brother in America. It had been translated from Gaelic to English, and spanned the years 1887 to 1910. Ryan held his breath when he came across a paragraph from a letter dated September 9, 1894.

Last night I paid a call to the cottage of Maurice and Maire O'Dunleavy. Old Maire if you remember has an uncommon gift with the storytelling, and many still pay calls to hear them told. The islanders are yet wary of the family though, for they're said to be shape-shifters, each and every one, even the baby in the cradle. I myself don't pay heed to the stories, for I heard that 'twas Maire's twin sister Cait* heard the call from the Lord himself all these years past, and is still living across the water in a convent there. Maire and Maurice are old now, and we are all waiting for them to be called to heaven. But they don't seem in a hurry to go, and are healthier than most. Indeed they might outlive me! Long lives are said to run in their families.*

And that was all.

The asterisk was explained at the bottom of the page: *Names have been changed to protect the family's privacy.*

Ryan read the paragraph several times. Then he turned the page. On it was a black-and-white photograph, with the caption *"Islanders take a break from earthing potatoes. Circa 1900."*

The group of six people stood in the field, with the sea in the background. The women wore long skirts and kerchiefs, and a man wore a cap and long, baggy pants. A donkey, his back laden with bags, stood nearby, and chickens were scattered about their feet. Ryan gazed at the photo, wondering if his new contact lenses weren't working right. He raised the book closer to his face. In the photo stood an elderly woman who looked like Cleona, only younger, and another woman who looked exactly the way that Aisling did today. A young girl stood at her feet, her big eyes staring calmly out at him.

Ryan, who once upon a time would have feared that he was losing his mind, knew exactly who he was looking at.

∞

Rose opened the take-out bag and removed the subs, an Italian sub for her and a meatball sub for Ryan. Ryan shoved the academic mess away from the food and opened the wrapper. Rose watched, mouth slightly ajar, as Ryan sunk his teeth into the end of the sub and gobs of marinara dripped from the sides.

"What happened to you over there?" she said softly. "You never told me a thing."

Ryan wiped his mouth with a paper napkin, and didn't answer. They ate in awkward silence.

"So why did you want me to come over?" she finally asked, crumbling the paper bag.

"I can't make sense out of it all," he said, his voice strained.

Rose sighed. "Why don't you tell me about your trip?"

Ryan stood up. "Would you like a beer?"

"Beer?" she asked. "I thought you hated beer."

"I used to."

Rose smiled, showing a deep dimple in her left cheek. "Why not?"

He pulled two porters from the refrigerator and sat down at the table again. They clinked bottles, and Rose said, "To Ireland, for giving Ryan sustenance."

The beer went down icy cold and thick. He felt a little better. He gathered his thoughts as best as he could. Then he told Rose about the old women and their deaths, about Aisling, about the cottage and Donal and Dorothy and even Wally. He tried to include everything he'd been told about the family, everything that he'd seen. He even showed her the paragraph and picture in the book, as well as the painting of the nun. After he'd put it all into words, it didn't seem as dreamlike.

Then, without telling the more intimate details, he told Rose the story that Aisling had told him their first night together, explaining the clan's "selective breeding" based on the genetics of the parents. According to the story, health and longevity had been prized among the ancient clan, and worthy mates were chosen for reproduction.

"She's putting you on," said Rose. "It's fiction. It has to be."

"I don't think so anymore."

"Love has infected your brain."

Ryan sighed, glanced at some papers in front of him. "It sounded like a kind of old Celtic eugenics scheme to me," said Ryan. "I once researched the idea as part of a report on heredity and genetics." He held up the old report for her.

"Let's hear it," she said. She took a deep pull of the beer.

"Both Plato and Aristotle believed in the city state's need for healthy citizens to make up an ideal society. Men and women were encouraged to reproduce when they were at the peak of their physical and mental powers, in order to conceive the healthiest and most intelligent children. In fact, the term 'eugenics' comes from its Greek roots, meaning 'good in birth.'"

Ryan knew he sounded crazy. He put his head in his hands and moaned.

"I see where you're going with this," said Rose helpfully. "Go on."

He straightened up. "Well, Francis Galton—he was a wealthy, intelligent half-cousin of Charles Darwin who actually coined the term 'eugenics'—wanted to maximize brilliance and prevent 'feeblemindedness.' Galton encouraged 'good' marriages that would produce highly intelligent males and assure the stock of the next generation. The Nazis, as you know, took the theory and warped it to their own ideas of an Aryan race, where people of certain Nordic traits—blue eyes, fair skin and blonde hair—should be favored over other 'inferior' races of people. This kind of reproduction hurried along Darwin's principles of 'survival of the fittest.'"

"So you're making a comparison to the early inhabitants of the island," she stated. "Same principles."

Ryan nodded. "Maybe the clan prized health and long life. Maybe they understood, even those thousands of years ago, that mating with other healthy, long-lived members would create similar offspring. Maybe over time, the clan members, isolated from the outside world, lived longer and longer lives, the likely result of a genetic mutation. And do you want to hear something *really* weird?"

"You know I do."

"The Celtic surname 'Owen' is from a Latin derivative meaning 'good offspring'! I think they took that name themselves over a thousand years ago, back when surnames began to be used in Ireland to distinguish the various clans."

Rose laughed so hard that Ryan could smell her beer-breath. "My dad is going to love this. I never knew you had such a creative side!"

Ryan ignored her. "A clustering of centenarians on islands has been seen before, you know, so the hypothesis isn't that far-fetched. Genetics and cultural isolation often produce astounding results," he claimed, pushing papers toward Rose for her to examine.

"Isolated islands, such as Okinawa and Sicily, have demonstrated a much higher number of centenarians than denser populations, right? They also tend to exhibit higher levels of inbreeding and clustering of genetic variants—which could be a bad thing," said Ryan. "But the genetic similarity, so far, hasn't been detrimental to those populations. On the Irish island, though, it seems that maybe thousands of years of purposeful mating caused too high a level of genetic similarity."

Rose still sifted through the papers, studying charts, so Ryan went on. "Over time, the intensive inbreeding would lower such an isolated population's ability to survive and reproduce, which would be consistent with Aisling's explanation of low fertility in her family."

"Like the cheetah," offered Rose.

"You know about the cheetahs?" asked Ryan.

"Yeah, I read a couple of years ago that the cheetahs are endangered because of their lack of genetic diversity due to thousands of years of inbreeding."

"Right," said Ryan. "And a long-ago population bottleneck that brought the cheetahs to the brink of extinction. They bounced back a bit, only to find themselves endangered again, presumably because of the necessity of inbreeding."

In the resulting silence, Ryan heard Rose's stomach hassle with its food.

"Aisling also told me that she'd only just started menstruating, at the age of 25. She said it ran in her family," Ryan said, shifting his eyes from hers. "And her mother Orla died from childbirth at the age of 58. I saw the dates on her gravestone."

"Holy cow," said Rose. "No wonder she passed away. That's too old to have a baby."

"Not necessarily," said Ryan. "I thought perhaps the late menstruation and conception was a result of the mutation in the genes. As the population aged, their fertility shifted forward to meet their demands."

Rose sat back in the chair and stretched her hands over head. "They sound like a new species, almost," she said. He knew she was humoring him. "Like something on the Galapagos Islands."

Ryan smiled, recalling the dreamlike visit from Harriet. On the Galapagos Islands, evolutionary biologist Charles Darwin had discovered plants and animals that had been seen nowhere else—and their nature often varied from one small island to the next, even though the basic volcanic geology and climate were essentially the same.

To Darwin, all of those species, stuck in their lonely

archipelago, had diverged from their ancestral stocks and then gone right on diverging. They had broken the species barrier.

"I'd have to examine more DNA," he said. "But I was pondering the same thing. The island has been inhabited for thousands of years. It's possible, I suppose, that the people on the island became genetically distinct from the rest of Europe. From the rest of mankind."

"But don't forget lifestyle, Ryan," said Rose, echoing her father and damping his enthusiasm. "These island people come from poor, hard-working stock. A trip to the market, to the harbor, to Sunday mass would burn hundreds of calories, not to mention all of the field work they used to do. It sounds like they ate a lot of vegetables and whole grain bread, with very little meat and lots of fish. And being so isolated, I imagine family and community were important to them. All of the storytelling kept them together. It's a prescription for long life out there."

Ryan agreed. Early on in his trip, he had factored lifestyle and diet into his analysis of the twins, and into his analysis of the island population as a whole.

"It's not like that anymore though," he noted. "Their diets are full of junk bought at the market—chips, cookies, candy, canned meat and fruits. They drink too much. I spotted a few satellite dishes. Their families are scattered across the world. The traditional lifestyle is all but gone. Aisling—and maybe a handful of others in the West Village—are the only ones that carry it on."

"Like Okinawa," she said sadly.

"The genes are still the same though," said Ryan. "They have the *capability* to live long lives."

They were quiet for a few moments, lost in thought. "I wanted her to leave with me," said Ryan softly.

"You did?"

"I didn't think she would though," he said. "And now, I'm glad she didn't come with me."

"Why?"

"The island needs her." It was the only way he could explain it, and by the way that Rose's eyes shone, he could tell that she understood him.

"The elderly on the island," said Rose thoughtfully. "Do you think they could have some kind of mutation in their genes too? Something that contributes to their longevity?"

Ryan smiled. "I see that I at least piqued your curiosity today," he said. "You know, at first I thought the other elderly on the island just looked old compared to the lack of youth. But I guess it's possible the genes could have been dispersed throughout the island—to those that have a family history there. It would take man power to get samples from them. Similar to what your dad and I did in Okinawa. We had to get the government's permission and fill out a bunch of paperwork. It would be a very public kind of thing."

He stood, and Rose stood too, her brown eyes searching Ryan's. "I guess I might as well tell you...the bone arrived yesterday," she said.

Ryan felt a spike of adrenaline that made his head spin. "Is it okay?"

"As far as I can tell, it survived the trip overseas and its holiday in the mail room." She searched his eyes. "Do you still want me to do the test?"

Ryan nodded. "You might as well."

20

———————

Three weeks later, on a cold January day, Ryan traveled to New Orleans to interview a centenarian, whose brother, also a centenarian, lived in the same house with him. They were both on a verified list of centenarians, a rare feat for male babies born in 1920 and 1921.

Their physician had sent the research study two buccal swabs, but instead of examining their DNA, Ryan had been filled with the desire to actually meet the brothers. They had been born in the South in the early twentieth century, after all, and they still lived on their own. Longevity, he'd been told, ran in their family.

King and Winston Jackson, 102 and 101 years old, lived in a small, white house on a tree-lined street of similar white houses. A clothesline looped through the backyard, and a wooden swing hung from the ceiling of the porch. Ryan thought of Aisling and the island as he rang the doorbell.

A young woman in a pink velour jacket and pants squeaked open the screen door.

She smiled warmly at him. "Hi, I'm Tammy. Come on in. The boys are ready and waitin'."

King and Winston were seated on an old floral sofa, their hands in their laps. Their dark skin and brown eyes shone youthfully beneath snow-white caps of hair.

"I'm Ryan Abernathy, from the research study. Thank you so much for meeting with me."

"Oh, we slipped you into our busy schedules," said Winston, his voice deep and powerful. "We are as good as movie stars these days, ain't that right, King?"

"Oh, sure," smiled King. "Just like Sammy Davis, Jr."

"Denzel Washington," corrected Winston.

Ryan settled himself into a comfortable armchair and removed his notebook and voice recorder from his backpack.

"So, how has your health been this year? Any complaints?" asked Ryan.

"Oh, we've got the arthritis," said Winston, holding up his large, knobby hands and rubbing them together. "And our hearing ain't so good. Tammy tells us we holler at each other all day. But other than that, we ain't got no worries."

"What's your favorite meal?" asked Ryan. Since he'd been back in America, he'd put on five pounds. Food, he'd learned, was more than calories.

The two brothers looked at each other and snickered. "Well, as you can see, Tammy cooks for us, and she makes chicken. Any kind of chicken dish in the world," said King. "This soda pop here is about the only thing in this house that don't have chicken in it."

"Beggars can't be choosers, now," Tammy called from the kitchen, where Ryan smelled chicken frying.

King fiddled with his hearing aid, then lowered his voice. "Tony—that's my grandson—brings us steak all cooked up every other day. Don't say nothin' now. Tammy would get her feelings hurt."

Tammy poked her head into the room. "Tony brings them their cigarettes, too."

The men looked at each other and burst out laughing.

"It's true," said King, shaking his head back and forth. "I tried to quit about 30 years ago, but you can't teach an old dog new tricks."

Ryan sat between them on the sofa as the two men showed him scrapbook after scrapbook. They featured a farm and a furniture store, and many children, relatives, friends. They told him countless stories from their lives, some of which were confused and conflicting but nonetheless heartening. Ryan didn't once check the time.

They showed him their yellowing birth certificates.

"Did you ever think you'd live this long?" asked Ryan.

"Mama and daddy lived to 100, both of 'em. So did their mamas and daddies. Ain't no surprise, I reckon."

"You outlived them all, though," pointed out Ryan.

"Yeah, I guess we did," admitted King. "Our wives too. All five of 'em."

King and Winston cackled, slapped their hands on their knees.

"And your children are getting up there too, isn't that right?" asked Ryan.

"They're all grandparents now," said Winston proudly.

Ryan looked down at his notebook. "Do you ever think about...passing on?"

"No, we never do," said Winston. "We just keep on livin', ain't that right, King?"

King nodded. "Yeah, ain't a nice thing to think on, that grim reaper sneakin' up on you."

"Better to concentrate on living, isn't it?" asked Ryan.

"Oh, indeed it is," King intoned, his face serious. "I just love life."

He then broke into the Louis Armstrong song, "What a Wonderful World." Ryan bit the inside of his cheek, to discourage tears.

"You alright, son?" Winston asked.

"Yes," Ryan choked. "You have a fine voice."

"That I do," Winston said. "Better than King's, anyway."

After sharing a meal of Tammy's fried chicken, biscuits and sweet tea, Ryan helped them out to the porch swing, despite the coldness of the day, and took several photos of the two of them, grinning and hamming it up for the camera. The photos were now featured prominently on the research study's website, along with several other centenarian siblings and their families.

Ryan wanted to meet every single one of them again and ask them about their long lives. He wanted to hear *their* stories, not just the stories that their DNA told. Their samples, which once would have been so appealing to him, still lay untouched in the lab freezer.

21

In early March, Ryan ran along the cracked sidewalk that skirted strip malls and office buildings, apartments and gas stations. He was passing a large church when the door to the chapel opened and a large group of black-clothed teenagers emerged, blocking his path.

"Sorry," he breathed, and ran around a red-headed female. As he passed her, he saw in her face naked grief, and he flinched, shoulders to his ears.

He forced himself to keep running, but after a minute or so, he doubled back on the other side of the street. He found a bench beneath a tree that faced the church, and he sat down.

A dozen mourners had gathered outside the church. Most of them were young, perhaps college students. They all sobbed openly, the crumpled tissues in their hands forgotten. Ryan guessed that he had stumbled upon the end of a funeral for one of their own.

He could see that the inside of the church was still packed with people. Funerals for young people always seemed to draw more attendance, he thought. As one got older, the list of available mourners grew shorter.

He also knew that the death of a youth was an unnatural occurrence, in these times of modern medicine and western progress. He wondered if the youth inside the church had died of a rare disease, or perhaps had been the victim of something more violent. The news of such early deaths tore through a community like a sickness itself, and mourners gathered together in a house of worship, grasping for meaning.

A robin alighted on the tree next to him, a harbinger of spring. And he saw that the tree had the tiniest beginnings of growth on its branches. Little whitish-green pustules bubbled on the dark wood, proof that life went on inside the tree. He thought the mourners inside the church would be happy to grow such buds on their own bodies, if it meant that all in life was not death and grief, that their lives, their joy and contentment too, would eventually bloom forth again.

He found the red-haired girl in the crowd, wiping her nose with a tissue. Her back wilted, giving her the look of a much older woman. He thought of the way that Aisling had appeared in the graveyard the day of Cleona's funeral. She had stood so defiantly straight, as if the island was hers to inherit. She mourned, yet she understood.

When he thought of her now, he of course saw in his mind a genetically gifted creature, a superior being, a scientific marvel. He knew without a doubt that she carried the promise of longevity in her blood.

But deeper, beneath the sheen of DNA gold about her, he saw her true essence, and it was much stronger—more lasting—than the titillation of longevity. He once would have been more than thrilled to study her, with no thought whatsoever to the girl herself. But now, he thought that just being in Aisling's presence, day after day, would bring him peace.

He got up from the bench and began to jog home, before the casket could be loaded into the curbside black hearse, biding its time like a giant vulture.

∞

Back in his apartment, he fixed himself a grilled cheese sandwich and ate it while checking his e-mail. The dozen or so emails were mostly updates from online health stores, except for one. He opened the email immediately, knowing that it contained the online results from the genographic testing lab. He stared at the computer screen, anxiety like a drug in his veins.

A month earlier, Ryan had removed a small brush from its plastic wrapping and scrubbed it along the insides of his very own cheek. He had sealed the swab in an envelope and mailed it to the lab that specialized in ancestral genographic testing.

The lab had analyzed his 46 chromosomes, half from his mother and half from his father. For each gene he had received two copies, one from each parent, and the copies had interacted with one another, except for two small pieces of the DNA—the Y chromosome, which was inherited from male to male, and the mitochondrial DNA, which was inherited from the female to her offspring.

The two pieces of the DNA had recently allowed geneticists to trace back a human's history through the mother and father to his or her founding ancestors. In fact, studying DNA mutations over time, it had become possible to trace every human being on Earth back to founding lineages, thousands of years old.

As he scrolled and clicked across the charts, he soon found that his maternal haplotype placed him in haplogroup U5, the oldest European haplogroup, with origins almost 50,000 years ago in the Middle East. It now included around eleven percent of the European population. Carriers of the haplogroup could be found especially in western Britain and Scandinavia.

His heart beat faster, as he moved to the portion containing his male ancestry. His paternal haplotype placed him in a haplogroup extremely common in Ireland, as well as in Spain and Scotland.

In some circles of research, it was affectionately known as the "clan of Oisin," after the hero who lived for a long, happy time in *Tír na nÓg*—the World of the Forever Young. Because the "clan" had traveled along the Atlantic waterway, forming families and communities, Ryan's male ancestors were most likely lovers of the sea and the coast, hardy and full of courage.

Ryan nodded to himself; he felt he had known the history, as soon as he'd stepped onto the white sand of the island. He had felt vital, more vivid, simply breathing the Celtic coastal air.

His mom and dad had raised him admirably, but now he could hardly recall what their faces had looked like. In his dreams, his mom appeared as a sickly, sad blur, not herself, yet he always awoke feeling fortunate to have dreamed about her at all. He couldn't remember what it felt like to have a mother, a person who actually cared whether your underwear was clean and your socks matched.

Life had plowed along, burying his memories beneath layers of time, so that digging for the memories of his mother and father, grandparents and brother, had left him grasping handfuls of useless dirt.

But he could let go now, in a way.

He sat back in his desk chair, glee percolating in his chest, instead of the anxiety that normally squeezed there. His DNA was alive at last. And the knowledge settled him, made everything alright. He *had* come from somewhere, a long line of ancestors that stretched back tens of thousands of years. All of their stories had merged together to make one new story.

Like Aisling's tales, his DNA gave him history that no one could deny, and he wanted to honor it by living the life he'd been granted.

He wasn't afraid for it to end; he was afraid that it would never begin.

∞

Every Sunday, Ryan stopped his run to sit on the bench facing the church. He liked to see how the church was used to celebrate the various stages of a human's life. One day he spotted a mother holding a baby, a long, white dress spilling over the mother's arm, proud father trailing behind. One day he saw a wedding party emerge from a white limousine, the shiny bridesmaids clutching bouquets of peach-colored flowers as they checked the hems of their dresses.

He also liked to see how the building itself changed its

appearance from week to week, depending on the light and the time of day. On an overcast day, the bricks of the church appeared as dark as blood, intense and judgmental. But on a sunny day, the mortar between the bricks glowed like molten silver, making lines of connection all over the façade that suggested mathematical perfection, a higher power.

He admitted to himself that there was something comforting about the church. He liked how the church itself connected family, brought people together, wove stories. And yet, he didn't feel the need to go inside.

His thoughts moved to a true believer, the Irish nun, Sister Ignatius. He wondered on her health; he feared that the cancer might have overpowered her by now. He wasn't pleased with how he'd treated her. He had tried to protect Aisling from a media onslaught, and in doing so, had humiliated Sister Ignatius. And she had known the truth about the family, even though her perspective on the matter—a miracle by the hand of God!—was a bit different than his own scientific outlook.

He hadn't been able to leap so far, to accept the fact that 180 years of age wasn't such an impossibility. Was it his lack of religious faith that he so easily doubted? Or was it the naysayers of the gerontological professions—the ones who'd declared that reaching such lofty ages was humanly impossible—who had wormed their way into his thought processes, poisoning his hope?

He wished that he could somehow contact the nun to tell her that he now believed, not necessarily in God, but in something magical.

∞

On his way to the mailbox the following day, Ryan stopped to look at the green shafts of daffodils poking stubbornly through the cold soil. The occasional drafts were still frigid, and yet, the spice of spring pierced the early April air.

He reached into the mailbox. Amid the usual magazines and bills, an air-mail envelope burned in his gloved hands. It was postmarked from Ireland and addressed to Ryan Abernathy, not to the study.

Inside his apartment, he opened it and found a carefully wrapped buccal swab. On a sticky note were scribbled the words *"Hope you can use these! An Irish lassie wanted you to have them. Dr. P. Fitzgerald."*

Ryan remembered to breathe. *Aisling had sent him her DNA.* The card felt precious in his hand.

Also in the envelope was another, smaller envelope. Inside it was a short, gray hair, the hair of Catherine Owen. He now had the samples he'd been wanting all along, samples that contained generations of very unusual mitochondrial DNA.

He saw himself in the lab, analyzing the codes, isolating a mutation, comparing the sequence to that of the old bone. He could see himself determining the mutation's part in the family's longevity. He could even see himself engineering that genetic sequence to concoct pharmaceuticals to increase longevity and health in the population at large. He saw himself grow rich; he had short, flat hair and drove a Rolls Royce.

Then he heard Aisling's voice, spinning stories long into the night. He thought he smelled the salty sea, the sweet scent of a turf fire, the menthol water of the stream. He imagined a flock of gulls taking off from the cliff side, pushing into the wind.

He forwarded the hair, the buccal swab, and typed

explanation to the longevity study, care of Dr. Buxton. Then he wrote a check, which almost drained the trust that had been created from his deceased parents' estate, and addressed an envelope to the person whom he knew would put it to better use than he ever could have.

He remembered to pack a heavier coat.

22

Sister Ignatius's back ached as she bent over the flower bed. The weeds had already begun to sprout alongside the nuns' prized daffodils, and this April they particularly bothered her. She pulled them out with a ferocious twist of her entire arm and tossed them over her shoulder.

She was angry with God. She had finally admitted it to herself while lying sleepless in her bed on a dark February night. He had forsaken her. She could usually see the reasoning behind God's actions, but as hard as she prayed, she couldn't understand the reasoning behind the taking of Sister Ambrose's life.

The timing of her death was no coincidence. He had taken her away, to serve no higher purpose here on Earth, where she was desperately needed. Sister Ignatius had truly believed that she was acting according to His instructions. Throughout the two weeks on the island, she'd hardly even felt like herself, and she attributed this to God's mighty hand in her life. He had been moving through her.

Mother Superior had believed her rebellious behavior—the calling of the reporters and the sharing of such personal information—to be a manifestation of her illness. But she had always been spirited, and God knew this. He'd told her to...

Dear Lord above. A wave of pain erupted in her head, deep inside it where no taut fingers, no medication, could possibly reach. Her entire body secreted perspiration, further dampening her already moist habit. She turned away from the flowers and retched into the pile of weeds. She wiped her mouth with a handkerchief pulled from the pocket of her habit and examined the vomit. It was mostly stomach acid, for she'd lost her appetite for food a while ago. She'd lost so much weight that even her coif didn't fit her head properly.

Sister Charlotte dropped a watering can and rushed over to her. She tried to pull Sister Ignatius to her feet, but she was having a hard time standing up straight. Her body wanted to fall backward, even though her brain knew that wasn't a good idea. Fortunately Sister Charlotte was a strong young woman. She was able to get Sister Ignatius to her narrow bed. She filled a glass of water for her and left it on the floor beside her.

Sister Charlotte's face pinched with worry. "I'm going to get Mother Superior."

Her rubber footsteps squeaked quickly down the hallway.

Sister Ignatius tried to focus on the two photographs—the only ones she'd taken on the island—taped on the wall next to her bed. One showed the ocean swirling against the cliffside, taken from above. She had been delighted to see how blue the ocean had appeared in the photograph—a holy blur of turquoise just below the surface. The other photo was of Sister Ambrose, lying in her bed with her eyes closed—the photo she'd shown to the reporters.

She had spent many long minutes staring at the photos, speaking with God, praying. But now, the photos wavered. She shut her eyes, then opened them and tried to focus again, but still the photos danced.

She shut her eyes again, and tried to take deep breaths, smelling the altar bread baking in the kitchen, the dirt on the sleeves of her habit. She tried to swallow, but her mouth was dry. Soon, she could hear Mother Superior's slow, purposeful stride coming down the hall. She heard Sister Charlotte stop outside the door; it sounded as if she were crying. Sister Ignatius didn't feel like opening her eyes.

She felt Mother Superior's dry hands fumbling with the veil and the coif. After a while, she got it all unpinned and lifted the cloth from her head, leaving the white skullcap that encircled her thin, gray hair. Sister Ignatius sighed at the relief. A cool washcloth was placed on her forehead.

"Is there anything I can do for you?" asked Mother Superior.

"No," she whispered. Even speaking that one word made her belly flip.

They were silent for a while, and Sister Ignatius could hear the blue birds singing in the meadow beyond the garden. Mother Superior turned the cloth on her forehead.

"You have received a letter. From America."

Sister Ignatius opened her eyes and tried to focus on Mother Superior. Mother Superior reached into her robe and pulled out an envelope. With a nod from Sister Ignatius, she opened the envelope and took out a rectangular piece of paper. There was no note.

"It's a check, written from the account of David S. Abernathy, in Virginia."

"How much?"

Mother Superior didn't answer for a long moment. "It's for 453,000 American dollars."

Sister Ignatius merely stared. She couldn't even recall the man's face, but she well remembered his passion for science.

"In the memo line, he wrote 'for the church on the island,'" said Mother Superior. "What does that mean?"

Sister Ignatius turned her head to look at the photos beside her bed. She could see the colors with perfect clarity, even with the tears in her eyes. Sister Ambrose's age-ravaged face grew into a garden full of daffodils, and she heard the hum of bumblebees as they danced atop the petals, then flew into a world where women were special, blessed, leaders of a religious community that grew in size with every passing day.

"The scientist believes me," she said. Her voice was barely more than a whisper, but in her head, it soared with joy.

God hadn't forsaken her at all.

23

———————

Aisling walked slowly down the road through the thick, April fog that had enveloped the island for two weeks straight. Most of the islanders still hunkered indoors, but Aisling was drawn outside, for the company of the island itself.

It felt good to walk, even though she was exhausted. She inhaled the viscous air, feeling the fullness in her belly that was a baby growing inside her. She imagined a small, red-haired child scampering beside her, occasionally reaching up for her hand.

When she reached the East Village, she stopped to rest on the misty beach. These days her rests had lengthened, even though she'd had to sit in the rain. She couldn't see very far in front of her. She listened to the water rush over the sandy shore.

At first, after he'd left the island, she thought he'd return, if not to her, then at least to the marvel of science that she'd spoken of. But then he'd stayed away too long, and she'd begun to give up hope. The doctor had told her he'd had some sort of electric mail address for Ryan at the place where he worked, but she'd shaken her head at him. The computers at the community center frightened her, and anyway, news of a baby shouldn't be made known on a screen.

She tried not to think of him now, the way that he'd looked at her, and touched her, as if she weren't even real.

She heard the honk of the horn as the ferry approached the harbor. She was surprised the ferry was even running in the fog. Someone must have paid the captain well, she thought.

She got up with some difficulty and walked toward Dorothy's hotel. Dorothy had taken Aisling under her wing after Catherine's funeral, and Aisling had grown fond of Dorothy, much as she would an aunt, or maybe even a mother, although she couldn't be sure of the feeling. Aisling now helped out with the cooking and laundry, sometimes the gardening. Dorothy paid Aisling a bit, so that she no longer had to turn so many sweaters to make ends meet.

Dorothy suspected the parentage of Aisling's baby, yet she never once asked Aisling about it. Instead, she loved to pat Aisling's growing belly, proclaiming it to be a girl. She'd given Aisling an old, brown crib that she'd stored away. She'd even found some old baby girl clothes and pink blankets that she'd washed and mended.

Dorothy had already promised to babysit.

Aisling arrived, damp and tired, in Dorothy's kitchen, where Dorothy was running a gigantic electric mixer.

"Ferry's in," yelled Dorothy.

"I heard," said Aisling. "Dirty day for running the ferry."

Dorothy turned off the mixer and stuck a spoon in the batter to taste it. "I don't have a reservation down," she said, licking her lips.

The two women stepped to a kitchen window that overlooked the harbor. Through the fog, they saw the punt being rowed through the water.

"Could be a government man," said Dorothy. "Checkin' on the school."

They stood there watching through the window for several minutes. After a while they heard the call of an American man as he walked down the pier toward the beach.

"Sure, but he sounds like a Yank," said Dorothy.

They looked at one another then. Aisling grew gooseflesh under the sweater and leather jacket, and Dorothy squeezed her hand hard. Aisling walked to the front door of the hotel and stepped outside.

Blinking against the moisture in the air, she walked to the edge of the water, still not able to see a thing through the mist. Time swelled around her, and through the fog she saw a man emerge. He had a mess of sandy brown, curly hair, but no glasses, and he wore a big black coat.

She watched as he continued to walk forward, the fog refusing to let him go. Then she saw him take her in.

"Aisling?" he called, his voice muted by the mist. His face had healed into a shape even more handsome than before.

"It's me!" she shouted.

He dropped his suitcase in the sand as he ran toward her. When he reached her, he grasped the back of her neck beneath her jacket with both hands and kissed her hard on the mouth. She would have slumped to the sand were it not for his strong arms now wrapping around her, feeling her lower back, her round belly.

He froze, pulled away from her to look at her stomach. "You're pregnant," he stated softly.

"Aye."

His breath came hard from his nose. He searched her face for answers, the same Ryan she'd known.

"You're the father," she said.

He ran two hands through his hair and then caressed her face tenderly, his hands smelling of lavender. "And...everything is progressing normally?" he asked, his voice cracking.

"I've been to see Dr. Fitzgerald once every month. He said the baby is growing."

"What about you?"

"I'm fine. He'll help me get to a hospital when it's time."

They stared at each other, the thick fog seeming to dull their words for a time.

"I never suspected this," said Ryan.

"You told me you understood how babies were made, from the farm."

He nodded his head, chuckling a bit.

"Why are you here?" she asked. The words sounded hard, but she didn't mean them to be.

"I missed you," he said. "Very much. Nothing is the same for me now."

"I think you miss the grave stones. The DNA in the bodies of my ancestors."

He laughed and pulled her toward him. "I thought of...*you.*"

"My DNA?" she whispered. "A strand of my hair?"

"No. Just you. Your stories."

They leaned into each other, forehead to forehead.

"But thank you for your cheek swab," he said into her ear.

"Did it help you? With your work?" she asked, pulling away from him to look him in the eye.

"No." He shook his head firmly.

"Oh."

"I quit studying genetics. I want to stay here with you. On the island," he said. "I think I'd like to be a farmer."

She felt the baby move inside her, and she placed Ryan's hands on her belly. His eyes grew round, and he grinned.

She was filled with hope. Perhaps she wasn't the last in the line at all.

∞

Ryan and Aisling finally sat down in the sand where they stood, continuing the stream of stories they had begun back in late October.

After a while, intrusive sounds came from the shore, as two mates from the ferry rolled a dolly of stones down the pier, shouting at each other in Gaelic. Out of the fog appeared Mother Superior and Sister Charlotte.

"Those are the stones for the new church?" called Mother Superior.

"Aye. We can't unload the whole lot of 'em ourselves though."

"We know of some able men who want to help," said Mother Superior. "I need to let them know the shipment has arrived though."

"Bless you for your patience," called Sister Charlotte, as the nuns disappeared into the fog.

Aisling turned to Ryan and said, "The ground was broken for a new church, near the ruins. The sisters organized it, but they won't tell me where all the money is comin' from. They come to me with all kinds of questions—paint colors and cushion fabrics and the like."

"Is Sister Ignatius here then?" he asked hopefully.

"No. She died not too long ago. From the cancer."

Ryan nodded sadly. "Catherine was a nun in her convent...all of those years ago."

"Aye," said Aisling. "I think that was why she left the island. She knew she was special—she'd heard the stories, same as Cleona—but she must have believed it was God callin' her."

"I treated her terribly that day. I regret that."

"You were tryin' to help us."

He leaned back into the sand. The sky was just a layer of mist, but he knew that blue sky lay somewhere beyond it. "That's going to something, watching a church being built here."

"Aye," said Aisling. "I've never seen a thing go up here except weeds."

"I just might go inside it, when it's finished."

"I'll go with you."

The fog seemed to disintegrate before her eyes, and the island around her was brought to clarity.

∞

In the cottage, the hearth burned more brightly than it had in years. Aisling and Ryan had finished a supper of fish and vegetable stew and were now tucked naked beneath two wool blankets on a duvet by the fire.

A painting of Catherine, completed the same year she had returned to the island, stood propped on a wall nearby. Her green eyes glowed in the light of the fire. Ryan had told her that Aisling would buy more of Old Pat Michael's paintings to hang on the white-washed walls of the cottage; he said that he hated to think of them gathering dust in the back of the market.

Now he pulled down the blankets and traced the curve of Aisling's belly with a warm hand. He then told Aisling in soft murmurings about America and the world he knew. He told of the recently watched movies he'd seen, books he'd read. He described airplanes, zoos, Mexican food, dog racing, the Blue Ridge Mountains, college dorms. He described different kinds of trees, the way some of them changed their appearance through the seasons. He told of far-off places with foreign names: Okinawa, Sardinia, Nicoya.

Aisling listened carefully, her eyes closed. The world beyond the island was dreamlike, at a distance. When he stopped, she begged for more, anything he could remember, no matter how small. The baby liked the sound of his Yank voice, she said.

His phone rang late in the night. She heard him get up to answer. She watched his buttocks as he stood with his back to her. He pulled back the curtains a little to peer out at the darkness.

"Rose?" he whispered. "What is it?"

The conversation lasted about five minutes. Other than a few words, Ryan was quiet the entire time. He snapped the phone shut and after a long moment at the window, came back to bed.

She rolled into him backwards, so that he could wrap his arms around her belly.

"Who is Rose?" she asked softly.

He took a moment to answer, rubbing her protruding navel with his thumb. "The doctor who was going to analyze your ancestor's bone."

Her throat suddenly tightened. "What did she want?"

"Well, she finished analyzing the bone today. She was calling with the results."

He pulled her body around so that she was facing him. His face wavered with shadow from the dying fire.

"The person in the grave was between 130 and 140 years old at the time of his or her death." His lips twitched and his chocolate eyes, without his glasses, were lit from within.

She already knew. "'Twas the grave of Sean, great-grandfather to Cleona and Catherine. He was a great traveler and treasure hunter. He'd come back with tales to tell, and whatever he found, he'd give to the islanders. He died without a penny to his name."

She laughed. "It's just like himself to give the precious bone away instead of keeping it for his own."

Ryan nodded, his face serious. "It's an incredible find—for many branches of science, not just genetics. Rose needed help performing the test. Now a great many people know about the find. I won't be able to keep the world from the island anymore. Or from you."

"It isn't your fault, Ryan," she said. "The island might do the world some good."

He kissed her tenderly. Then he said, "Tell me about Sean."

∞

As dawn arrived, Ryan read from a book of poetry, recently published by an Englishman called Wallace Rose. The poems had been written during the author's brief visit to the island last autumn, and Aisling could see why Ryan liked them.

His voice faltered when he read one he liked, called "Island."

At twilight she whispers to me
She is old, the sea in her eyes
Her breath skips, a girl
barefoot on the rocks, once
And she won't last the winter, for
her corncrake cry
goes unbidden, no eggs
She is empty house
untrod sand
Secrets freeze on her tongue
and night comes, full of gull's noise.

She shivered, and wrapped her arms around Ryan, her belly resting between them. They slept deeply, and Aisling again dreamed she was the corncrake. At last, she had heard the "crex-crex" of the male, back from holiday in Africa and looking for a mate; when she had peered into her nest, she had seen an egg there, a speckled oval of promise, and the grinding of the tractor blades was almost too far off to be heard.

The sound woke her, and she jolted up, still half-asleep. She looked out the window, and realized that the noise had been made by a steady stream of men, pushing and hauling dollies and wagons along the road by the cottage. She heard the nuns' voices cutting through the cool spring air.

"The church will be small," said Mother Superior. "But this stone is the very best."

"Aye," agreed Sister Charlotte. "It will last for centuries."

Aisling closed her eyes, adding yet another part to the story she'd heard when she was just a young girl. She would tell it to her own child one day.

ACKNOWLEDGMENTS

This novel was originally published as an e-book by Diversion Books in 2013. Its subject of longevity grew from my keen interest in extending my own life (in order to avoid death!).

But a lot has happened in my life, and in the world of genetic sequencing, since its original publication. Any inaccuracies of a scientific nature are due to either my own mistakes or the ten-year gap between the original publication and this slightly updated, self-published version.

For this version, I'd like to thank my birth mother, Lori Jerden, with whom I connected shortly after the book was published. The theme of adoption, and the resulting absence of background health information, appears in the novel, and I was more than a little anxious about her reading about all of that in the book, because I thought it might have led her to believe that I was somehow unsatisfied with certain aspects of my life.

Which I wasn't—I was adopted by two wonderful parents (the late Norman and Patricia Schnell) who gave me the stellar upbringing that she believed she couldn't at that time of her life. But through the years, I've been so happy to find that Lori is a loving, fun, ultra-cool, patient, and well, a badass ex-Navy woman, and I know that she somehow understands the life of the writerly mind and how we have to write about the very things that force us from our comfort zones.

So thank you, Lori, for your willingness to connect and cultivate a relationship with me, and thank you to my husband, Sean, and to my children, Dorsey, Katherine and Ellery, who traveled to Ireland with me for our first overseas family trip right *after* this book was published. You'd think I would have tried to make the trip *before* writing a book about such a special place, but thank goodness for other writers who'd already written such wonderful books about Ireland, both past and present, that I thought for sure I'd already been there.

So thank you from the bottom of my heart to you writers as well. May your words live on, for eternity. Slainte!